KILL

MW01170594

The Poetic Theory

Marshall 'YA'POET' Pope

Popes Inspiration Publishing

KILLUMINATI_ The Poet Theory

ISBN: 9781092973618

Printed in the USA by Popes Inspiration Publishing

TABLE OF CONTENT

Ch. 10 The written truth 107

INTRODUCTION

Knowledge and understanding were the key motivators behind writing this book. After careful analysis of the scriptures, it was one I found quite favorable.

Hosea 4:6

My people are destroyed from lack of knowledge; 'because you have rejected knowledge, I also reject you as my priests; because you have ignored the law of your God, I also will ignore your children.

We have consistently rejected following the Most High and chose to follow the ways, tradition, principles, and ideology of the world. We have replaced the doctrine of what Elohim teaches us for the doctrine of the world. We're become of the world allowing habits, traditions, and mindsets to cloud the judgements and views of what's important. This book will renew your mind and break the restraints that's used to control and hold our minds in bondage.

Our crowns been snatched from our heads and replaced with a sense of false power. Traditional thinking has blocked out reality replacing it with illusions that leaves us vulnerable to deception. We quench the holy spirit when we praise worldly leaders instead of our creator. The deceivers of this world couldn't prevail if we chose truth over deception.

James 4:4

You adulterous people, don't you know that friendship with the world means enmity against God? Therefore, anyone who choose to be a friend of the world becomes an enemy of God.

We must set ourselves apart from the world and stop seeking acceptance while looking for leadership and friendship in deceivers. You can strengthen your walk with Elohim if you stop allowing stumbling blocks to change your path.

Colossians 2:8

See to it that no one takes you captive through hollow and deceptive philosophy, which depends on human tradition and the elemental spiritual forces of this world rather than on Christ.

Mainstream religion teaches how to be a good slave to world leaders. Scales on our eyes have blinded us for centuries keeping us from seeing the truth in plain sight. This book provides you with truth and understanding while exposing secrets many don't want told; so, renew your mind and hit reset.

Romans 12:2

Do not conform to the pattern of this world but be transformed by the renewing of your mind. Then you will be able to test and approve what God's will is; his good, pleasing, and perfect will.

CHAPTER ONE

SCIENCE

Science have been presented to the world as a cure and justified remedy. The science council.org defines science as the pursuit and application of knowledge and understanding of the natural social world following a systematic methodology based on evidence.

Science is the opposite of faith. Hebrew 11:1 defines faith as the substance of things hoped for and the evidence of things not seen. Therefore, if faith is the evidence of things not seen then science is the evidence of things seen.

Most scientist don't believe in God based on a study in 1998 called academy of science. Before the 17th century science was known as Natural philosophy. The term science is just a more modern term. But the biblical scriptures warned us about believing in science. Colossians 2:8, beware lest anyone cheat you through philosophy and empty deceit, according to the tradition of men, according to the basic principles of the world, and not according to Messiah.

Movies have altered our brain to believing the world will end with a meteor falling or perhaps aliens will come to earth like in the movies. In films man use tools to fight back in preventing the world from being destroyed. Their movie themes are similar to the towel in Babel in which man built to fight God's wrath.

In the time of the Greeks the Israelites said that God created the earth and everything in it. But a man name Aristotle the most influential philosopher during that time said the world must have existed from eternity. A direct challenge of the belief God created the heavens and the earth.

In 17th century the scientific revolution began with philosophers putting science up against reason. We have fallen for deception in our never-ending quest for knowledge. But we must take the same advice the apostle Paul gave to Timothy:

1st Timothy 6:20-21

'O' Timothy! Guard what has been entrusted to your care. Turn away from godless chatter and the opposing ideas of what is falsely called knowledge, which some have professed and in doing so have departed from the faith.

Many strayed away from the faith seeking knowledge. Science is one of the adversary's ways of helping society grow away from God. People trust medicine and science before trusting God. If we follow the money trail behind modern science, it will lead us to John D. Rockefeller. This man represents one of the powerful families related to the Khazar Ashkenazi Jews. The Rothschilds, Rockefellers, Carnegies, and Morgan's are families that use their money and influence to dictate worldly affairs.

The Rockefeller family are the main influencers of the scientific and medical community. John D. Rockefeller is known as the father of modern medicine. Modern western medicine is not like it was in biblical times. Doctors once practiced healing through the natural because our Father gave us the natural resources to give our bodies what it need to heal. With natural and herbal medicines, we were able to live healthier lives. In the early 1900's doctors were using these natural medicines till the 20th century then all that changed. John D. Rockefeller one of the richest men in America was the main component behind this change. During the 20th century Rockefeller nearly owned 90% of all petroleum refineries in America through his company Standard oil corporations. His Standard oil company split into smaller companies like chevron, shell, Mobile, Exxon and etc. which made his family even richer. However, in the 20th century scientist began using petrochemicals to create a variety of compounds from oil. After extensive research it was discovered that drugs could be produced from petroleum. Since John D. Rockefeller controlled the market of petroleum, he was able to use his influence to change the medical industry. One of his first power plays was buying IG Farben one of the largest chemical and pharmaceutical companies which is now known as Bayer.

Rockefeller hired a contractor known as Abraham Flexner who submitted a report to congress in 1910, known as the Flexner Report. This report stated that there were too many doctors and medical schools in America, and that all the natural healing methods that existed for hundreds of years were now unscientific quackery. This meant that medicines used for thousands of years were now considered alternative and the new petroleum base drugs was now classified as gold standard.

In order to gain even more control, Rockefeller took more control over the American Medical Association. Using the Flexner Report he got Congress to change laws related to medical practice. With these legal changes Rockefeller teamed up with Andrew Carnegie and started funding medical schools all over America under strict conditions to only teach their curriculum. This way of teaching excluded the teaching about herbs and natural treatments only focusing on the medicine Rockefeller was in control of. Dieting and teaching about non-drug treatments were completely removed from medical programs. Medicine was changed from wellness and prevention to just simply treatment.

We allowed the treatments our Father gave us for healing to be replaced by what scientist gave us. Over time if anyone challenged this change, they were silenced till eventually everyone started doing precisely as they were taught. After removing traditional medicines from schools Rockefeller launched a smear campaign against his competitors using the media. Soon Allopathic defined science based was the only system of medical teaching to increase the process of prescribing patented drugs. When evidence came out that petroleum-based drugs were causing cancer Rockefeller then founded the American Cancer Society in 1913.

There is no explanation due to information being suppressed nor prevention for Cancer just treatment. History's been rewritten to exclude the truth behind the lies told to society. Elite families such as Warburg, House, Wilson, Aldrich, Morgan, Vanderbilt, Schiff, and Rockefeller hid themselves in plain sight behind powerful corporations exerting their power through them. Their names are never discussed when we talk about Big Pharma totally unaware of the truth. Rockefeller empire along with Chase Manhattan Bank known as JP Morgan Chase owns over half of the pharmaceutical interests in the United States.

The Rockefeller university pride themselves on being able to use science to dominate, control and spearhead modern day medicine. Modern day medicine is laboratory made to push us further away from depending on God to depending more on man. Laboratories are also credited for making most of our foods, and the meats we consume are actually cloned. We must stop depending on man and turn back to God for our survival. We must be hungry for the word of God and willing to eat the truth. Once we taste the truth, we will spit out the lies and only digest what God prepared not what man made for us.

GOD MADE

I'm not self-made, man-made, nor illuminati made but God made so I give my Father the glory…

Because before I had the leading role in my scripted life He already predicted and foretold my story!

Every word from my anointed pen is prewritten and every step in my life is a predetermined destiny…

I'm remade from the ashes of my previous life into the Phoenix from my Father's own special recipe!

Crafted from blessings, molded by fire, and designed in the image of a mirrored reflection of Father…

I survived death by the protection upon my flesh through the baptism of love mixed in holy water!

The world cannot change what God made but what God made can change the world's prospective…

People don't sell your soul to the elite in response to the lies and false images the media projected!

We were not descendants from apes nor was the earth created from the thesis of a big bang theory…

Scientist are brainwashed technologist with their man-made machines designed by Satan's tyranny!

From the dust of the earth, we were created by He who vanished the enlighten one for his vanity…

In the image of the Most High, I am God made sent to kill illuminati for breaking the oath of humanity!

We have been tricked to believe technology enhances civilization when in truth it programs slaves...

After the temple fall the Phoenix shall rise from the ashes of reconstruction because I am God made!

LAWLESS ONES

Eternal secrets revealed to man by fallen angels of ancient
times has once again been exposed...

We have allowed lawless and ungodly ones to trade us
information in exchange for our souls!

Our quest for knowledge has driven us farther from the truth
as we embrace the Father of lies...

One small step for man, one giant leap for mankind is
humanity's sin and reason the earth cries!

I sympathize with my brother Enoch for he warned us against
following the lawless ones advice...

Yet we allowed these mystic beings once again influence over
the most high's plan for our life!

Technology has corrupted our minds and contaminated our
spirits with viruses and programs...

The whole world is now controlled by a computerized evil
sent out through emails and spams!

Distracted by social media with clones, fake news and sex has
invited Satan into our homes...

Laws have been passed and bills have been signed while we
unbeknownst accept and condone!

The terrorist have already entered in the back while we are
watching the front totally unaware...

We must Killuminati known as the lawless ones in hopes to
prevent another holocaustic nightmare!

HOLY VACCINATION

Pour me a glass of wisdom and fix me a plate of knowledge so I may dine with intellectual salvation...

Another weapon of mass destruction was created in a lab by the government to wipe out foreign nations!

Casualties will be sacrificed in making America great as they experiment with science, life, and physics...

For the survival of this country a nationwide purge was granted to balance and rid all unwanted statistics!

On the calendar of humanity, we only have a lil' time left before Yeshua returns and reclaim his throne...

Ebola, Aids and Corona are all man made & government approved to undermine the laws written in stone

Khazars are Turkish Russians from the synagogue of Satan making false claims to my Jewish heritage...

If the church is the bride and Yeshua is the groom, then I must be the best man in this unlikely marriage!

Trump the uncanny tyrant has taken on the role of Caesar predicting and dictating foreign trading policies

The united states is indebted to China so therefore the strategic move is cutting ties with foreign colonies!

Gentiles are intelligently clever in manipulations and diligently skillful in exploiting an enemy weakness

We fear death, sickness, and the truth but not the God that brought you out of Egypt!

15

Ebola, Aids and Corona is no match for the holy vaccination that triumphs any lab experimental virus...

So, if you feel like shouting, dancing, or crying it's just the holy spirit of the elected one sent to inspire us!

CHAPTER 2

POLITRICKS

In order to subdue a nation, you must first control the minds of the population. The voting process give people illusions they have control over an elective official. Many are tricked into believing that they really have a voice when actually they're puppets being controlled by puppet masters. The platform you think you're standing on is really already sold to the highest bidders, the rich and powerful elite known by many names such as the Khazars, the seed of Esau and the Rockefellers.

Voting is really a national censor allowing the elite to have some knowledge of how you feel regarding their decisions. We view the world through lenses that makes it comfortable for us rather than face true reality. People are scared to live in the truth because its easily to live in the traditional lies. Change is hard for the majority of the world because we're comfortable with the way things are rather how things could be. We have been deceived by distractions like material things, wealth, and fame to keep us from achieving the truth. The world is viewed and also divided by the rich, middle class and the poor; 3 different levels of people. We must view the world through a pyramid structure starting at the base going up till we reach the top. If we use the base of the pyramid as people and go up the pyramid; the amount of the people become smaller till its only one person standing at the top.

Every level of the pyramid should be looked at with different motivators on each level. You will be surprised to find out when you reach the very top money is not even a motivating factor. The top of the pyramid is where all the decisions about this world is made and at the very bottom is where you will find money as the motivating factor because they are the ones without money. The ones at the base of the pyramids are poor so they think money will make their life better therefore they commit their lives to moving up toward a higher level. The middle of the pyramid is where the middle class resides and are viewed as a level of success. Their motivating factor is more success, fame and also wealth but not at the top. Power and knowledge resides at the top of the pyramid and because they already have everything; money is not a factor.

If we use this same pyramid as a world view, we will think the top of the pyramid is where the president sits but actually that's not true. Presidents are only front men for the real decision makers of the world sitting at the top of the pyramid. A president's job is to read speeches, give interviews and take photos with world leaders. The presidency is just a high-level position as a front man being told what to do by the real leaders of the world. Their speeches are written for them, and their remarks are already prepared, so are the press conferences that appear to be real. These presidents are an illusion of a leader called figureheads which means a nominal leader or head without real power. They are distractions making people believe they're making decisions but in reality, they are taking orders from those at the top of the pyramid. Behind the curtains are the real leaders, hidden like the producer of a news program or a television show. You only see the anchors or actors but not the ones guiding or leading them and telling them what to do. The ones you see are not the ones in control, they're only script readers.

The reality you really want to see is only an illusion to keep the real puppet masters hidden. This illusion keeps those in power in power and those without power without it. This method allows them to control us and use us as pawns as long as we allow them to manipulate our thinking. We're behind as a nation in truth and facts therefore if you are behind, you can't lead only follow. We are distracted by things we like rather than the things we need.

Social evolution have masterfully tried to cypher what 400 plus years of slavery could not do. We have been led to believe that suddenly black lives matter but truth is we are being distracted into thinking struggles are subconscious thoughts. Education, politics, and power is controlled by who controls the money. Mental imprisonment keeps the population in order and destitute into believing that they freely have a choice when in reality their thinking is being programmed.

Definition of Democracy is a government by people which in terms means the rule of the majority or a government in which the supreme power is vested in people and exercised by them directly; or indirectly through a system of representation usually involving periodically held free elections.

The elected ones who really run the world need the people to think they really have power, so they give them a voting system. In the ancient world power was only held by a chosen few called kings, queens, and emperors. Their power was able to be seen making us aware who wielded this power and control. We accepted their rule as a divine right from God called a monarchy which means a form of government which the power of the king or queen is hereditary. This was the seen hand of control during that time rather than the unseen hand we have today.

During the time of Yeshua, we were run with an abstract form of government by earthly leaders; but in today time we operate like the matrix. The matrix is a world that has been made to purposely deceive you, while at the same time it influences you to contribute satanic energy to help establish a new world order.

We have been given the illusion of power, but our minds think we have been empowered and that's how we are controlled. They will not implement this new world order by force instead a more subtle approach is gracefully applied. The biggest part of implementing their plan is to empower the people with an illusion of power. If the world felt, they were being forced with this new world order they would rebel against it.

The plan is making people think they have a voice and a say in the way the world operates. Making the people feel they have a voice makes them feel empowered. Leading the people into feeling they have choices makes it easy to lead them into saying what you want them to say. The church is a good example of how people are manipulated by withholding truth and only giving them the part, you want them to play.

Christianity is the tool used to coerce people into believing false doctrine dictated by hypocrites. We're taught our voices are the power behind our votes when really its basically considered just a process of brainwashing.

Oligarchy is a combination of wealth mixed with persuasion. The same laws that are meant to protect us are used to control us. The political system was not designed to actually give us a voice but merely designed to know what we are thinking. Our votes do not elect candidates; our vote only exposes our thoughts on what we think about the candidates. These elective officials are already hand-picked and chosen by the unseen hands of wealthy families behind the scene. If we follow the money trail; it leads us directly to the real decision makers behind the scenes making decisions.

The presidents and other elected leaders are only the front men or puppeteers taking orders from their puppet masters. The money holders behind the scenes hold more control than your vote for the candidates that were placed in the front positions. Politics doesn't give power to the people; it merely steer the hearts and minds of the people into believing they have a voice. If you must vote then vote for God, choose God, and serve God

IDOLATRY

I am your God, but you choose to idolize your precious statues built only to honor a hateful past...

So, whomsoever place themselves above or before will not be first instead you shall be last!

The time of the serpent has come who will poison the gentiles once again with lies...

He will influence worldwide genocide with his war talk of hatred and racial divide!

Do not be an idolater my children you must serve the lord and let the pagans worship the idols...

Do not follow the arrogance of an idiot who's only power is based solely on a title!

Simon may amaze the people and pretend he has all the answers to every question you ask...

But he who place himself on my throne will surely face my unmerciful and undeniable wrath!

Rebellion is a sin therefore waving a rebel flag shows supreme dishonor to my holy nation...

Only united may you stand in heaven and whomever fights for division will be placed among the damnation!

So, tear down all your shrines of sin like the son of man cleaned out my church...

For I am not a statue of Idolatry but the Most High God the father of heaven and earth!

21

You will find no fault in me to wander astray worshiping false Gods and man-built idols...

Slavery is a history you should be ashamed of my lost children not idolatry to feel proud of!

I am the holy mountain Dr. Martin dreamed of and on my eternal ground every man, woman and child are free...

I am your God and I forbid idolatry therefore I condemn anything that represents hate, racism, and bigotry!

HITLER FOR PRESIDENT

They orchestrated Trump's election regardless of votes to
show politics is their power source…

Politicize the whole world by giving them false platforms to
make them think they have a voice!

What's the difference between a republican and a democrat
but scripted lines of pretense tension…

Actors in suits hell bent on deceiving God's children with
corporate entertainment and religion!

The Senegal of Satan controls the media and all forms of
public relations concerning information…

Hitler for president is no difference than saying America is
only great for one race the Caucasians!

Was the holocaust a great atrocity or did our German brother
discover the truth about Satan seeds?

We were taught Hitler's a racist by more racists unsympathetic
toward America's slave caustic greed!

In 1940 he wrote a revealing letter and produced a film
unveiling the true identity of the real Israelites….

To bury his findings, they placed his symbol and quotes
behind supremacists to empower the whites!

We accepted our conqueror's religion, obeyed our captives
laws, and ate the crumbs they feed us…

Yet we still remain stiff necked idolaters intent on biting
God's hand every time he freed us!

They gave us Obama to shut us up then they turn around and gave us Trump to put us in our place…

Next election I vote Hitler for president because I know his fraudulent enemies are the ones I face

WHITE OUT

The art of war is winning without conflict by confusing the
enemy with different forms of attack...

Like mental warfare which breaks an opponent resistance till
they have no Will to fight back!

The best way to destroy a race of people is by convincing
them to destroy themselves with self-hate...

Feed them democracy then starve their ambitions by snatching
opportunity off their plate!

White out Christian religion so they will think Yeshua was a
blue-eyed Italian name Cesare Borgia...

Next program their minds with technology using the internet
to create a computerized world order!

Eliminate their leaders by assassinating their image, their
character and exterminating their funds...

It's like committing murder without firing a shot and no
evidence of a gun!

The presidents or should I say the front men are merely
puppets hired by the governmental elite...

God bless America or will it be the first to burn when heaven
rain fire on them for being the greatest thief!

Operation 'white out' has been exposed and the descendants
of fallen angels has been revealed...

Negros you have been identified as black Hebrews from the 12
tribes illuminati forced out of Israel!

We must remain true or suffer the same fate as our enemies
who have gained power from lies...

Killuminati for thinking they can dominate a whole world by
using politics as their disguise!

ANTI-CHRIST OR SATAN MISTRESS

Anti-Christ or Satan mistress for president which one do we choose?

One screams hate and the other whispers it so whoever win we still lose!

Neither can judge or criticize the other nor will you find a black kettle in neither kitchen...

Ain't no truth amongst liars in this friendly presidential game of competition!

We have identified the devil's whore and his bastard child as they plan to inflict genocide ...

This worldwide struggle over power is the first step toward a worldwide future divide!

The embodiment of evil has been awakened to cast his ugly shadow upon the earth...

As it is written in the book of revelations hell will impregnate the planet and eventually give birth!

This deceiver will deceive many as a peace maker with global influence of bringing peace...

This false prophet that comes to power on a platform of lies will be directed by the beast!

Out of the sea of nations promising prosperity as a great political leader for all mankind...

Will it be Anti-Christ or Satan's mistress that robs the faith from a world that is already blind?

He will be worshiped by many as they marvel at his lies, hate speeches and racial quotes....

While Satan's mistress wears a false smile, display false love, and make promises of false hope!

Leader of the New World order and the head of a one world government will be their claim...

But no title can these two imposters be rewarded ever out rank the name above every name!

God is my ruler, my king, my leader, my creator, my Father, and my president...

Therefore, I will follow no man or no woman only he who was heaven sent!

CHAPTER 3

INTERNET

Let's start with the word television and add program which reads television program. It actually means exactly how it reads; the television is programming our minds. For hours we sit, watch, listen and absorb whatever we're watching till our mental energy drains. Our time was occupied with the mental brainwashing of watching television till it was replaced by an even more effective means of brainwashing, the internet.

The internet slowly became the fastest and most addictive world consuming method of brainwashing. It cast a shadow so big that it makes the world look small. The more people interact with the internet increases its popularity and value. The internet is based on the same business model television is based on which is really monetizing attention through ads. Over time we allowed ourselves to become data to be studied, monitored, and monetized.

The primary job of most social media sites are to gather more data about us so they can sale us more content. We are targeted by the advertisers whom our data is sent to. Facebook and other social media sites are considered free sites to mingle and interact with people all over the world. But in hindsight we give these social media sights a virtual version of ourselves. With ever click, like and swipe we are being recorded and studied to learn more about us. Once our virtual identities are established everything we do online is being tracked and monitored.

Technology has consumed humanity and tricked us to become slaves with their self-titled smart devices. Unknowably we have given control of our freedom and our will over to being pawns of technology. Anything called smart is a data collecting device used to monitor the population and sale ads back to us. We have been outsmarted by devices created to manipulate you into believing you can't function without it. Let's take for example smart phones called iPhone, these are the bestselling phones in the world. Most of the world either owns an iPhone or another high-tech brand but still a data collecting phone. We been manipulated to allowing the elite watchers to monitor us by these cell phones.

We live in a time of mass deception learning from the humility of finding out everything we thought we knew about this world are lies. Governmental coverups gives false information to keep us inflated with not knowing. The internet's predicted programming is shaping our morality with indoctrinated mind controlling. Our social lives have been altered from physical contact to cyberizing. We are now suffering from the effects of indoctrination which is defined as the process of teaching a person or group to accept a set of beliefs uncritically. That means what's taught is learned and accepted as facts

The writers of history with their indoctrinated thinking and their narrow-minded views of events use the internet as a foundation for their source of information. The internet is a tool fully created, controlled, and operated by the Khazar Jews from the seed of Esau. We can't ignore the facts this love/hate relationship stems from two brothers who represent two different nations.

We have been monitored by certain individuals using devices like iPhone, computers, and the internet to hide behind and create mass deception because of bloodlines. Race wasn't a factor till one man introduced skin color into the equation, Johann F. Blumenbach a white supremacist from Europe. Johann was the very first person to divide humanity on the basis of skin color. Although he didn't create racism, he simply placed the classification system that is still used today. His work is considered to be one of the influential works according to race. But underneath the mass conception that black people are hated because of skin color is a misconception, it was our Hebrew bloodline.

Joseph Arthur de Gobineau is another man that had similar belief as Johann F. Blumenbach. In the 19th century Joseph also believed the white race was superior, he was known for his influence on legitimizing racism through the scientific racist theory. He was credited for developing the theory for Aryan master race. This distorted hatred have been translated by the rise of technology to spread faster. Social media has adopted a new way to spread hate and manipulation upon the world and control the masses.

Anytime you log onto a social media site, information on every keystroke is fed into powerful computers somewhere. Algorithms in these computers correlate this data. They compare you with other people with similar profiles, The algorithms is a process or set of rules to be followed in calculations or other problem-solving operations especially by computers. This process experiment with ways to use this information to modify your behavior so you will do what they want. What they usually want is for you to respond for an ad for a particular product or service. But they can be trying to influence you to vote or not vote. We must be alert and mindful of these harmful effects of social media like blatant addiction and manipulation.

It's sinister how these big digital media companies use algorithms to discover things about you that you haven't revealed directly. Their business model involves finding the ways of attracting and holding our attention so that we can be influenced by advertisers, politicians, and other paid clients for their purposes, not yours. A vast amount of data is collected about you, including your facial expressions, the way your body moves, who you know, what you read, where you go and what you eat. This data is then used by algorithms to create feeds of stimuli ads or posts that's designed to boost your participation and increase the effectiveness of advertisements. Facebook representatives and executives have written they deliberately incorporated addictive techniques into their service, which is why the honest terms would be 'addiction' and 'behavior modification stimuli.'

Advertising has evolved considerably from printed media to digital media. In the printed media, advertising was mostly a one-way street; the advertiser sent forth the ad and hoped for the best. In the digital media, advertising accompanies the connections that people have and change their product accordingly. The way advertising works in social media involves monitoring the user closely, to measure the effect of what is called an ad so that a personalized stream of stimuli can be incrementally adjusted until the person's behavior is finally altered. Most social media customers are now living in automated virtual Skinner Boxes which are laboratory chambers used to study animal behavior. These skinner boxes were named after B. F. Skinner.

On social media, positive stimuli conveyed might include being retweeted, friended, or made momentarily viral. Negative stimuli include familiar occurrences of being made to feel unappreciated, unnoticed, or ridiculed. Positive and negative online stimuli are pitted against each other in an unfair fight. Positive and negative emotions has comparable ultimate power over us, but they exhibit crucially different timing. Positive emotions typically take longer to build and can be lost quickly, while negative ones can come on faster and dissipate more slowly. It takes longer to build trust than to lose it. One can become scared or angry quickly, but it takes longer for the feelings to fade. The sour and lousy consequence, which no one foresaw, is that the negative emotions are the most often emphasized, because positive ones doesn't get any attention.

The elite behind this technology use these services to manipulate ordinary users and society.

Another problem of social media comes from its role as a major gatekeeper for news. What this means is that more and more of us will enact with this because we only like news that pushes our psychological buttons. We enjoy violence and what's considered bad over good news and positive discussions. Most of this material on the Internet generated by people who are not what they pretend to be, or by computers and distributed on a mass scale by robots.

The Internet could be a means of bringing people together, but we rather engage in violence, anger, paranoia, conspiracy theories and fake news. Social media feeds you stuff that is intended to stimulate your emotion, and it is easier to stimulate feelings of anger, fear, and resentment than it is feelings of joy, affection, and security. This is a very deeply rooted problem that really needs to be addressed before it continue to alter the whole world and lead us further away from God. We have totally allowed ourselves to be distracted, manipulated, and controlled by the corrupted seeds of Esau who has undermined the whole world with their hatred for the chosen people of the Most High.

THE PLOT

In the 70's a baby was born from the aftermath of revolution
to inherit the struggle of his ancestral parents...

He suffered malnutrition from the truth which deprived him of
a healthy birthright and inheritance!

Every citizen is assigned a number from the government as
security that you may be identified in society...

Your birth certificate is your written censorship, and your
death certificate gives them authority to clone your body!

Advance technology is used to outsmart the masses by
downloading brain cells till your minds are empty.

Everything has a price even social media that's buying up
souls by the billions without paying one penny!

YouTube has replaced television shows while Facebook has
become our main source of communication...

The world is so preoccupied with media drama that has us
brainwashed with lies and falsified information!

My poetry has made me a target so I must remain hidden
behind poetic parables and incoherent truths...

I remain a victim of slander behind a tarnished image in hopes
to silence the voice of old and new!

The plot to assassinate my character has given me life beyond
death and the reason to live again...

What couldn't kill me as Marshall only made me stronger as
the Phoenix to get back up and win!

34

KILL ILLUMINATTI

I ran out the backdoor of hell to the front gates of heaven
begging Father for forgiveness...

He handed me a pen as my weapon against illuminati and said,
'go my child and kill this!'

Just as Enoch tried and Jesus tried so must I expose this
twisted plot to overthrow the King...

Scatter and enslave the Hebrews was part of the plan to trick
us with their lies and schemes!

Once we discovered our humanity, they found a way to appeal
to the beast in mankind...

After 400 years of wandering the earth lost, we allow hate to
control our hearts and mind!

Brother against brother and sister against sister in physical
warfare yet the real fight is mental...

The beast has taken his seat amongst the powerful and elite
and it wasn't presidential!

Technology has brainwashed us to think we hold the controller
when we are the robots...

We keep our eyes glued to iPhones and computer screens but
who is really being watched?

Is it a race war or a spiritual war that's killing more blacks or
it just a televised illusion?

The real murderer is illuminati, and their weapon of mass
destruction is called confusion!

The government has us under surveillance while they lurk in
the shadows of secrecy…

They got eyes on the moon but couldn't give you a description
if someone kill me.

Conversations have been recorded so I speak silently through
this anointed pen…

We must kill illuminati before it spreads its world domination
of mayhem and sin!

CHAPTER 4

HOLYDAYS

The Merriam webster dictionary defines tradition as handing down information, beliefs, and customs from word of mouth of one generation to another without written instructions.

Mark 7:13 Making the word of Elohim of no effect through your tradition which you handed down. And many such things you do.

Let's take for example holiday traditions in which we take part in every year however the scriptures doesn't speak on these pagan traditions. The real biblical Israelites took part in such days as the feast of unleavened bread, the Passover and other days considered holy. Later years the word holy days was later changed to holidays and the pagans started their own traditional days like Christmas, Easter, valentine, and Halloween to lead us away from the Most High.

We have been miseducated by traditions and indoctrinated with lies that has deceived us for generations. We have forgotten God's commands. With traditional holidays we serve him the same way the gentile nation serve their pagan Gods. When it comes to these traditions, we afraid of what the world thinks if we chose to walk along and not give in to traditions. We rather obey the world rather than the Most High. yet God warns us not to listen, obey nor love the world

Matthew 7:13-14 "Enter through the narrow gate. For wide is the gate and broad is the road that leads to destruction, and many enter through it. But small is the gate and narrow the road that leads to life, and only a few find it.

We spend money, time, and energy in celebrating holidays but not celebrating God. Generations have tried to convince us that these holidays are actual divine celebrations.

Colossians 2:8 'Be careful that no one takes you captive through philosophy and empty deceit based on human tradition, based on the elements of the world, rather than Christ.'

The scripture clearly explains that the celebration of holidays are the traditions of men not Christ. No one knows Yeshua's birthday, yet man nominated December 25 as that day calling it Christmas. We're told not to follow the ways of the gentiles and that's exactly what we did in following the gentiles traditions.

Christmas was practiced long before Christianity was classified as a religion and before the early church was formed. People would celebrate December 25th as the day of birth in regards to sun gods. This is the day when it is believed that the sun-god is reborn. Many of the practices, customs, and rituals that stem from this day are all pagan. The Romans celebrated Saturnalia, a festival dedicated the sun god Saturn, that ran from the 17th to 24th of December. This so-called festival included activities like giving gifts, orgies, and drunkenness.

When Christianity was adopted by Rome through Constantine, it did not replace their customs, it was infiltrated and corrupted by paganism. Only those who held true to the word of God and did not accept the Roman's worldly twist were able to withstand. The early church objected the celebration of Christmas. In the time of Constantine, Christianity was on the rise. There were many riots and uprising due to conversion of pagans to Christianity. Rather than react violently, Constantine claimed he had a vision about Yeshua's cross and that's the reason for him being in power. He later declared Christianity as the Roman's Empire's official religion.

While it seem that it was a win for Yeshua & Christianity, it turned into something quite worse. They held the First Council of Nicaea where they decided on doctrine, practices, and customs that would go along with Christianity to allow the already pagans to continue their same worship, but have Christians feel involved. Catholicism was born, which is the use of Yeshua intermingling with the idols and religion of mystery Babylon. It was here where it was decided that along with Easter, another pagan holiday, that Christians would worship the birth of Yeshua on December 25th, along with their sun-god Saturn. They named it "Christ"- "Mass" They discussed the customs and practices. It was a perfect solution for Rome cause they were able to continue with their pagan gods worship. Christians felt if they were able to worship the birth of Yeshua it was tolerable, but some Christians felt that was false.

Once this tradition started for Christians in the 4th Century A.D.; it was passed down through centuries over 1500 years becoming a practiced holiday all around the world. It's a tradition by man accepted as an official national holiday. However, much is to be considered when reviewing the history and meaning associated with Christmas.

You feel you are worshipping Yeshua on Christmas regardless of what anyone thinks but we are not to worship God in the way we want, but how He wants. When the children of Israel were freed from Egypt and built their idols in order to worship God, Moses quickly tore it down. They were commanded not to worship Him as the Pagans and Gentiles did. We should always worship Yeshua exactly the way he commands. The only way you should celebrate Christmas is if it's found in the bible but if it's not, then it's a tradition of man.

Jerimiah 17:9 'God looks at our hearts. And He sees that it is filthy, and wicked above all things.'

The Bible tells us that using traditions to worship God is an abomination to him. But people like to create god in their own image and worship him in ways that he tells us are not acceptable to him. There are clear verses that show offering things to him are considered insults to him; like Cain's offering was not acceptable. Aaron's two sons offered strange fire and were burned up. The children of Israel made a golden calf representing the God that brought them out of Egypt and were almost consumed. If you keep the traditions of man, then you are making the commandments of God.

Deuteronomy 12:30-31

Take heed to yourself that you are not ensnared to follow them, after they are destroyed from before you, and that you do not inquire after their gods, saying, 'How did these nations serve their gods? I also will do likewise. You shall not worship the Lord your God in that way; for every abomination to the Lord which He hates they done to their gods; for they burn even their sons and daughters in the fire to their gods.

THANKSKILLING DAY

He spoke with a malice tongue, but he could not provoke
anger in the indigenous man...

'Peace brother', said the Indian 'no need for greed the Great
spirit has divided the land!'

'Let us feast together and I will show your people how to
farm, hunt and ways to survive'...

In return the white man offered a peace treaty of false
friendship handwritten in deceit and lies!

A celebration of brotherly bonding became a night of murder,
rape, and execution...

We shall conquer every race of color and call it the United
white man's Constitution!

Christopher Columbus discovered preoccupied land and
declared himself the rightful owner...

After accepting the indigenous people hospitality, he murdered
every child, man, and woman!

Let us celebrate this victory with a toast and we shall call this
feast a day of thanksgiving...

Now that we have conquered the brown man let us white out
their history by raping their women!

The truth has been covered up for centuries with their media,
newspapers, and hypocritical lies...

The natives left a trail of tears soaked in the blood of the 200
slaughtered humans Columbus deemed uncivilized!

This day of celebration is really a day of mourning as we feast in remembrance of killers, butchers, and slavers.

I hereby declare atonement for this thanksgiving massacre based on the truth not the lie they gave us!

THE MERRY LIE

Christmas was a pagan festival passed down as a traditional holiday about a holy birth of salivation...

Yeshua known as Jesus was born at Sukkot according to John 1:14 so who are you really celebrating?

During the Feast of Tabernacles, the word became flesh bringing joy into a world of saints & sinners...

Some say his birth was in the month of September, yet we glorify and celebrate the 25th of December!

Jerimiah 10:2 warns us not to learn the ways of the gentiles, yet we follow man and ignore scripture...

Each year we celebrate paganism and Nimrod's birth using a false white imagery of Yeshua picture!

Banned by the early churches in the 1700 long before we adopted this blaspheme as a holy holiday...

Jerimiah 10:3-4 gives descriptions of a tree decorated by deceit spoken of by none other than Yahweh!

Disobedience and the lack of knowledge have rendered my people blind sinners with no direction...

The Christmas tree is an idolatry symbol for the sun god Nimrod's mystical rebirth and resurrection!

The spirit of Christmas is really the father of lies dressed as an angel using trickery of a false tradition...

Read Mark 7:13 before the whole world is deceived by Satan and his wicked paganistic superstition!

43

Saint Nicholas along with Black Pete warned kids to be good
or this demon would put them in a sack…

This enslaved Hebrew inspired the Grinch and Blackface
when whites would paint their face black!

Consumers saw profit in this merry lie, so they use media
outlets with large advertisements each year

Transforming Saint Nicholas into a fat white man in a red suit
landing on rooftops with magical reindeer!

This merry lie of paganism and Christianity has deceived the
whole world of morals, facts, and truth…

White Christmas is really just a cover up for the festival of
pagans not the holy black birth of Yeshua!

EASTER TRUTH

We have inherited paganism from the pagans by accepting
their unholy rituals in our holy beliefs...

Easter has reinnervated into a global celebration for Yeshua in
place of the ancient day sex feast!

Instead of orgies we hide eggs, attend church service and dress
in our new suits and flower dresses...

How does Ishtar the Goddess of sex symbolize a bunny rabbit
on the day of our saviors resurrection?

Will we suffer the same fate as our ancestors for worshipping
false idols or will our sins be pardoned?

They say earth dies in the winter to be reborn in the spring
giving new life to the flowers in the garden...

They place kids on the forefront in hopes we overlook the
truth they so skillfully buried behind myths.

I say, 'give back to Rome what belongs to Rome and let us
rectify with the God we pledged allegiance with!

We have been deceived far too long my misguided brothers
and sisters for us to continue walking blind...

We must Killuminati which dates all the way back to the
pagan misconceptions during the Roman times!

Easter has been the center point many Christian scholars at
one time considered the Passover for Jews...

But we all know the ones disguised as the Hebrew Israelites
are really the synagogue that Satan use!

I do hereby declare this day a pagan day as the rest of the pagan holidays we been fooled to celebrate...

The truth about Easter is bunny rabbits can't lay eggs, but you can be deceived a lying snake!

WHITE FRIDAY

Black Friday was once a day for white slave owners to sale
their slaves at a discounted rate…

Now the truth is considered a myth like all the other pagan
holidays we so happily celebrate!

This country is soaked in the blood of my people from the
forced labor of my ancestors hands…

Europeans have plundered, raped, and stolen our place in
history all for greed, power, and land!

Hear me oh Israel my stiff neck brothers and sisters you no
longer serve the decedents of Esau...

God scattered us to the 4 corners of the world as divine
punishment for not obeying his law!

May the tribe of Juda recognize they are the seeds of Jacob
and remember their Father Abraham…

We are the mighty Nation of Israel whose king's name is
Yeshua so behold the sacrificial lamb!

Give not yourself over to paganism nor worship idols or
celebrate days that mock our plight…

Black Friday is not just a bargain day for merchandise but also
a day humans were sold half price!

We must stop accepting lies and supporting falsified holidays
in the name of pagan traditions…

Black Friday is really White Friday since they're the ones
benefiting from enslaved colonialism!

CHAPTER 5

THE MIND

The most high God said: My people are destroyed from lack of knowledge. Knowledge is power therefore if your knowledge is diminished, your power decreases. We have been guarding our conscious mind and leaving our sub-conscious mind vulnerable and unguarded.

By sub-conscious programming we're consistently deceived by the television media, internet, and deceivers. Computers was created in the image of our brains to function by programming data. Psychology is the study of the mind to learn how the brain functions in order to manipulate it.

Our sub-conscious minds are automatically trained by repeated subliminal messages manipulating our thought process. The definition of subliminal is 'below the threshold of sensation or consciousness; perceived by or affecting someone's mind without their being aware of it'. Subliminal messages are dually designed to influence and manipulate our mental processes and behavior. The sub-conscious of your mind is programmed by consistently hearing or seeing something repeatedly over and over.

We think it's our intuition, but it's been programmed through various media outlets to manipulate our brains to remember what we read, watch, and hear which plays upon our ignorance to being mentally brainwashed. Over time we have allowed this deception of the mind to become active in sex, violence, language, and our spiritual beliefs. The mass media use music, movies, video games, television, sports, and the internet to influence our thought process.

Global elites with secret societies have used their manipulating devices to control the mental mindset of the world. Their favorite blueprint of manipulation is to hide the truth in plain sight. For example, let's dissect the single eye displayed in a pyramid on the back of dollar bills. The symbiotic eye is called the all-seeing eye. We see this symbol, but rarely do we study the hidden meaning behind it.

Some may call it a third eye symbolizing it as a representation of wisdom but if we analyze and research it more, we will find it was once referred to as the eye of Lucifer. Yet some religious scholars refer to it as God's eye watching over mankind. But the biblical God of creation is not the God they are referring to when they say the God of this world. The eye symbol represents light, and spirit often referred to as the mirrors of the soul. This symbolic eye was used to represent secret and occult wisdom to the Egyptians.

In Egypt it's said to be a reference to the eye of Horus the sun god as an ancient symbol of royal power. This single eye was once painted on the side of Egyptian funeral caskets in hopes it would enable the corpse to see on their dead journey through the afterlife. We have become too easy to manipulate and control because we do not know God nor obey his laws.

Matthew 7:22-23

On that day many will say to me, 'Lord, Lord, did we not prophesy in your name, and cast out demons in your name, and do many mighty works in your name?' And then will I declare to them, 'I never knew you; depart from me, you workers of lawlessness.'

We choose worshiping and celebrating the Lord in ways we desire instead of how he told us to. We have become custom to following the ways of the world instead of following our creator; we rather follow his creation. I live with a mindset of being set apart and not following the false illusions of man's traditions. I don't care about what they're arguing over in politics, I only care about what they all agree to cause I refuse to play political dissensions.

The media program our minds to interfere with our moods, their programming system has been able to tap into our emotions. When they want us to feel anger, they show us nonstop programs about racism. When they want us to panic, they create world atrocities and when they want to program us, they flood the news stations with their brainwashing news coverages.

The urban black communities has been shaped by their black films exploiting gangs, homosexuality, and drugs. Every black movie must include those three key ingredients in order to be successful. The ultimate goal is to push the real Israelites farther and farther from Yahweh so the curse of Deuteronomy can never be lifted.

Critical thinking and self-thoughts is beyond what the masses are telling us and considered to be uncommon behavior. The majority of people in the world don't think for themselves therefore it gives opportunity for others to use their minds.

Covid 19 was a global pandemic created by scientist to reduce the population. Right before this pandemic occurred a census was sent out to urban communities in poor neighborhoods and middle-class neighborhoods. The whole world was shut completely down as we watched loved ones die daily. Vulnerable and defenseless we were forced to call on Yahweh for assistance once again. Then once the pandemic created to exterminate the Israelites began to waiver we were struck with outright racist attacks. Although we are separated in geography, we are together in spirit against the spiritual warfare that plagues us.

We can't stop what's coming but we can try to prepare for what's coming before it officially arrives. It's time to start being proactive rather than just reactive. We need to focus on what's important in our lives and apply mental capability to achieve that goal. The definition of mindset is 'the established set of altitudes held by someone which is a mental attitude and a fixed state of mind.

Whenever you fully engage with the world you are being mentally attacked. The same way we exercise to make our bodies strong we must do the same with our mind. The mind control techniques used against us to weakens our brains till we become like walking zombies. We are being neutralized without even knowing we are being attacked. The unspoken battleground of your enemy is your brain so we must protect our minds at all cost. If you can control the head, then you can control the body so be aware.

Romans 8:5-6 Those who live according to flesh have their minds set on what the flesh desires but those living accordance with the Spirit have their minds set on what the Spirit desires. The mind governed by the flesh is death, but the mind governed by the Spirit is life and peace.

Colossians 3:2 Set your affection on things above, not on things on the earth.

The enemy has created a society where you must interact with the world in some way whether it's work, school or even the grocery story. The magnitude of this communicational control has no reset button so we must interact with the world in order to survive. Our school systems only teaches what they want us to know; and to think the way they want us to. The more you hear a lie it becomes the truth to you eventually.

The news no longer meant to keep you informed, its used to keep you sedated. We must stay convicted in the truth if we really want to survive in this world. The worst times are not behind us but rather ahead of us. It's imperative that we don't get distracted from the truth regarding manipulation and mind control so allow this scripture to guide your mind state.

1st Peter 1:13 Wherefore gird up the loins of your mind, be sober and hope to the end for the grace that is to be brought unto you at the revelation of Jesus Christ

BLACK PUPPETS

Let's give them a leader and place the words in his mouth we
want him to speak…

We shall call him our dancing puppet because we are the ones
controlling his feet!

Let's give him a platform and pretend he's anti-Semitic to the
white man's rule…

We will break his back by making him carry our burdens like
a good obedient mule!

Let's give him a name like Farrakhan or make him a gang
member called Nipsy Hustle…

Maybe then they're forget that dam Malcolm X and Tupac
ranting about the struggle!

We're put his face on every media outlet and make him a well-
behaved Marcus Garvey…

But he better stick to the script we give him, or we we'll tax
him like Steve Harvey!

Our puppet black leader will outdo any letter Mr. Willie
Lynch every wrote in his life…

Now that's how you break a whole lot of niggers by turning
one sell out into a sacrifice!

We're give him a few dollars and let him move in our
neighborhood thinking he one of us…

And if we decide to use a female black puppet then she can
satisfy our chocolate lust!

53

We fooled them with our politics, paganism, and a false doctrine of religious propaganda…

We even got them thinking their history is ours by using their own people to program them!

AFTER 400 YEARS YOU STILL MY SLAVE

Mr. Khrushchev predicted a takeover without firing a shot and ended with 'we will bury you'...

They have controlled our destiny, our minds and our children including our revenue!

The best tactic of war is distraction written by Willie Lynch with his divide and conquer...

I identified you as the lost tribe of Israel and not the African American presumption!

Every race is united, yet we allowed ourselves again to be brainwashed and hoodwinked...

Now we are targets because we refuse to jump from a leaking slave ship that's bound to sink!

Father warned us about idol worshiping and yet we still idolize our former masters...

Underneath disguises we hide our heritage and laugh at each other like a pack of jackals!

The bucks are impregnating women by the dozen, and they call it pimping nowadays...

I bet every white, red blood American is laughing saying 'after 400 yrs. they still my slaves!'

'Give me liberty or give me death' said Patrick Henry but all we ask is 'where the weed at? '..

Malcolm X tried to lead us, but the black Nation of Islam decided we didn't need that!

We followed Martin Luther King to the mountaintop but after watching him fall no one dared to climb...

And now we honor his memory for 28 days seeking the same solution to racism that he couldn't find!

America enslaved us, America hates us and now America has declared war on the black race...

'After 400 years you still my slave' that's what Donald Trump told us to our face!

UNMASKED

I have seen thy face of my enemy and he bears a striking
resemblance to me....

We may have the same ancestors, but we are branches from a
different family tree!

We both originated from Africa but from what tribe were you
produced?

African kings sold black Hebrews into slavery therefore
Yahweh chosen Israelites are my roots!

I was in bondage for 430 years in Egypt before being enslaved
400 years in America...

Israel was my first home before the Romans invaded and I
escaped to West Africa!

I was disinherited by my Father and cast away in ships for
disobeying his command...

False idols called fallen angels was the reason for my denial to
the promise land!

We have suffered pharaohs wickedness, survived the middle
passage, and endured white man rules...

We have been given many identities from Anglo Saxons,
Africans, and black Jews!

The bible describes our holy savior with hair like wool and no
indication he was white...

Yet Leonardo Da Vinci painted us Cesare Borgia as our
depiction of Yeshua known as Christ...

Though your feet were burnt like brass they rather display you
as an Italian Roman catholic...

And I am told to sing songs to celebrate my captivity like the
star spangle banner classic!

May my journey draw me nearer to thee by the steps I have
taken in the past...

My lord I stand before you naked from my transgressive sins
and finally unmasked!

LOAD YOUR BRAIN

It takes a whole village to raise one child, but we must first raise their awareness on education...

Each one teach one about the worldwide holocaust that began with segregation!

They say our kids are lost but I found our youth by using simple mathematics...

60 percent are incarcerated, and the other 40 percent are being used for target practice!

'I will not surrender my dignity' said Malcolm X so instead they hired black men with no pride...

'Get your hand out my pocket' said the nigger assassin before committing a black-on-black homicide!

Slavery was started with blood money so may it end in bloodshed...

56 bodies was the start of a revolutionary movement that ended the day they cut off Nat Turner's head!

One bullet in the face turned a mountaintop dream into a hillside nightmare...

Rest in peace brother Martin hopefully after the next 400 years we may finally make it there!

Load your brain with knowledge and words of wisdom in the chamber ready to speak out at the sight of injustice...

It is not always the white man my brothers and sisters sometimes it's just us!

The government teaches separation through politics so love me for me and judge me by my character...

Load your heart with God and aim toward change because every precious life matter!

CHAPTER 6

THE BIBLE

The holy bible is the best-selling book in the whole world. The king James version contains 66 books, while the catholic bible contains 73 books, and the Ethiopia orthodox bible contains 81 books. In order to be included in the official bible called a canon the books had to be considered divinely inspired by the word of God. who decided what books were included and excluded is decided by kings, religious leaders, and the ones in power with the most influence. This canonization of the bible excluded certain books that were considered too controversial.

Certain books that made it in the canon had strong backing from powerful and influential people while other books that may have been accurate and true did not because they didn't have that kind of backing.

Politics and economics played a major role to preserve the power of the church. In the mid 1800's many bibles including the King James version contained a number of books that has been edited out, these are known as Apocrypha. Apocrypha means hidden things which were either hidden books or secret teachings. These apocrypha books was not accepted as part of the official canon. Some of these books talk vividly about the history of Israel after the New Testament period. Any books that contradict the books that's accepted and believed got casted out and labeled heretics and the writers were condemned.

The book of Enoch written by a man that walked with God and was taken up by God. Enoch is one of few people mentioned in the canon who never died a physical death but instead was taken by God. Although his book didn't make it in the official canon,

61

his writings is still considered to be believable and sought-after. As a devout follower of God, it is said Enoch sat with the most high and then exposed secrets about humanity in his book.

Between 300BC and 100Ad is the time period in which the book of Enoch was written. Before the 4th century the **book of Enoch** was removed from the Hebrew bible and discredited. In his book he wrote about the renegade angels God sent to watch mankind called the Watchers but instead of watching mankind they lusted after the women. These angels sometimes called the fallen ones taught men war and how to make weapons while teaching the women about cosmetics. These same angels fathered off springs children called Nephilim; these Nephilim's are said to be one of the reasons God flooded the earth. The most high wanted to rid the earth of these abomination giants that were corrupting and attacking humanity.

In Nag Hammadi upper Egypt around December 1945 a group of farmers discovered a jar containing 52 religious texts written between the 2nd and 4th century. Christin scholars believe they was hidden there by a religious group known as the Gnostics; therefore, this hidden treasure were called the gnostic gospels. The Gnostics was a religious group considered to be followers of Yeshua; the Gnostics were said to have secret knowledge given to them by God. These religious texts that were found by the Gnostics contained **the gospel of Phillip, the gospel of Thomas, the gospels of the Egyptians and the testimony of the truth.**

In 367 AD, bishop of Alexandria name Athanasius declared the gnostic gospels to be heresy and threatened whoever read them will suffer the fires of eternal damnation. However, he did allow 27 gnostic gospels to be kept; and the 27 are the new testament.

The gospel of Thomas tells what Yeshua taught privately while the other 4 gospels in the new testament tells what Yeshua taught publicly. The 4 biblical gospels speaks on immortality of

Yeshua while Thomas focus more so on the humanity side of Yeshua.

The gospel of Mary Magdalene was discovered also in Egypt in 1896 along the Nile river. This gospel was written around the 2nd century AD by an unknown writer. Mary spoke on a relationship with Yeshua in an intimate way. In this gospel it also states one of the apostles said, 'Jesus loves her more than us.' This book also tells about holy secrets that was shared with only her from Yeshua which made the disciple Peter angry and jealous. Mary is best known as the apostle that witnessed Yeshua's death as well as his resurrection. 2000 years of tradition was overturned by the gnostic gospels and exposed the downplay of women during that time period.

The gospel called the testimony of truth gives a more vivid and different story about Genesis. Around the 1st century AD is when this unique gospel was written. In this book it also tells about God's wife Asherah, mother of heaven.

In the New Testament the book of revelations written by the apostle John describes the end of days and tells about Yeshua returning to earth. This book almost didn't make it into the New Testament like the apocalypse of Peter which didn't make it in. The apocalypse of Peter was the gnostic gospels with similarities to revelations. Some church leaders believed the apocalypse of Peter belonged in the new testament more than the revelations. Written in the 2nd century AD the apocalypse of Peter was one of 20 books of revelations kept out of the new testament. In Peter's apocalypse book he gives a guided tour of heaven and hell where Yeshua reveals to Peter the gruesome consequences of sin. In the book Peter's shown places where people are being punished for their sins on earth and so liars are hanged by their tongues over eternal flames. Women who have seduced men by braiding their hair to make themselves look attractive are hanged by their hair over eternal fire. The journey through hell is considered extreme in the scary apocalypse of

Peter while depictions of Yeshua's resurrection is considered downright very bizarre by church scholars. Peter's apocalypse speaks of Yeshua emerging from the tomb with a cross emerging from the tomb after him. God ask the cross 'where have you been and what have you been doing; have you been preaching to the souls that have departed?' The cross reply 'yes' which simulates the cross walk and talk at Yeshua's resurrection.

Also, in the banned book by peter called the gnostic apocalypse of Peter displayed Yeshua as a man who laughs in the face of his own death. In the book it say Yeshua show Peter a crucified man on a cross then shows him a laughing man on a tree. Yeshua tell Peter that the real him is the laughing man on the tree and not the dead man on the cross. This text is trying to tell us Yeshua did not want us to focus on the crucifixion.

We will never really know why some books were included in the canon and why some were excluded. The canon may be divinely inspired but it's been tampered with by men for centuries.

Around 1947 in Qumran located on the northwest shore of the Dead Sea in what is now known as the West Bank tucked away in an ancient cave 7 antique jars were found filled with strolls later named the Dead Sea strolls. The strolls reveal handwritten religious texts even older than the biblical texts we call the old testament. Written in Hebrew, Aramaic and Greek material is what we prefer to as sacred history and the cornerstone of faith.

Many biblical scholars has questioned whether Moses is the author of the 1st five books in the old testament since the bible was written after creation; and there weren't really any eyewitnesses during creation.

Translation of the bible to English were both religious and a political movement. Many prominent scholars that died were labeled as heretics for translating the bible to English.

In 1604 King James recruited 47 scholars to work on an English translation of the bible, the king James version. Later certain individuals left England to escape the tyranny of King James taking with them his version of the bible which became very popular in America.

Although many people have used the bible for many different and selfish reasons, slavery was the worst. In Genesis 9:22 was blueprints for whites to enslave black people. In the 1800's this incorrect interpretation of the bible was used to explain that awful injustice done to the black race. They say this unjustified act of sin led to the bloody civil war and divided the country. Greed, power, along with bigotry camouflaged the identity of this sacred book called the bible for centuries. Trimmed, cut, and reworded yet however hidden in plain sight we have discovered the true identity of the black race who we now know are the Israelite people Esau tried to erase from history.

THE REJECTED SCRIPTURE

He walked in the footprints of our Father and spoke the truth
suppressed by lies...

From my anointed pen drips the blood of Enoch giving my
words life through his eyes!

Oh, Father who is this righteous man that is rarely mentioned
in the cannon by the scribes?...

He spoke so vividly of the 200 fallen angel's oath to take the
daughters of man as their wives!

They taught seduction, lust and war with their technology
fueled by misguided temptation...

Their half angel half human offspring of giants attempted to
corrupt your beautiful creation!

Their sins were disobedience mixed with hate for the precious
humanity you so loved...

It was your first sons children the Nephilim's thirst for death
that led to their demise in the flood!

Scientific minds discreetly preserve the demonic technology
that scholars secretly keep hidden...

They replanted the seeds from the apple of knowledge that you
already once strongly forbidden!

For 300 years he walked with Father becoming the inspiration
for future biblical writers...

Among the dead sea scrolls we discovered the truth that
influenced the new testament in our bible!

The great grandfather of Noah who written words paints a
story better than any picture...

Enoch walked with Father, and he was not, for God took him
so all is left is this rejected scripture!

YESHUA

They have whited out my image and blotted out my true name
to represent their Christian monologue...

How can wooly hair like lamb and skin like burnt brass
resemblance a blue-eyed blond hair white God!

Catholic churches stamped their mark on religion and
spreaded their false doctrine of lies worldwide...

My name is Yeshua, and my Father name is El so by no other
name will I recognize!

Now that the truth is revealed to man the gentiles of Esau says
it doesn't really matter…

If it didn't then why you change, hide, and enslave my
disobedient children to whom I scattered?

I the Father, son and holy spirit speaks as one voice through
the pen of my poetic Israelite son...

Verily verily I say let not my words be used to justify sin,
condemn nor judge my chosen ones!

My bloodline has been tarnished and mixed with the seeds
from foreigners of heathen and pagans...

Passover has been passed over and replaced with paganistic
holidays to mislead like the curse of Canaan!

I shall return to reclaim my people from the four corners of the
world in lands they were adjourned to suffer...

Israel shall be a nation again, but I will not allow brothers
against brother, sons against fathers nor daughters against
mothers!

There will be peace instead of war and I Yeshua shall be your reigning king when I bring you home…

But by no other name shall I answer accept the one my Father gave me when I take the throne!

CHRIST-NOT

Deuteronomy 5:8 'Thou shalt not make thee any graven image
or any likeness of the Most High God Elohim...

Yet mostly every black family has a picture of a white man on
their wall calling him the king of kings!

It started with Ham's descendants the Indians then Shem's
seeds the Israelites which are the negroes...

Now they aiming at the Chinese but before that they targeted
the Mexicans for buying up all the stores!

Some of you black people could be leaders for our people
instead of just standing still and being targets

They asked Trump 'how many will die?' and he replied,
'enough for us to clone then refurnish our black market!'

So, before you hit the wow mojo sign and start testifying Oh
my lord this man is talking about Jesus Christ...

I ask you to read for yourself and let go of what grandma
taught because the one who taught her was a racist white!

Why don't pastors teach the old testament instead of preaching
the same scriptures from the new testament?

Thou shall be a humble servant to the gentiles and show
absolute support to their president!

What is Christianity I asked a Christian and he replied
following the teaching of Jesus Christ our Lord...

But what if I told you his name was Yeshua, and gentiles felt
empowered to name tamper with the son of God!

Jesus the Greek name you call is Yeshua in Hebrew which is your origin not the two countries used to describe you...

African Americans you are Israelites from the tribe of Juda so wake up and understand they lied to you!

I place my faith in God and my loyalty to Yeshua which makes me a trusted believer in the most high...

The Cesare Borgia worldwide imagery along with the name Jesus is Christ-Not just another historical lie!

I AM NOT A CHRISTIAN

Give to Rome what belongs to Rome which is their whited-out
version of our Israelite messiah…

Catholic churches have given power to the gentile races with
their false truths and wicked desires!

Spoiled seeds of Esau mingled with the offspring of Japheth
and the seeds from fallen angels...

The daughters of man were dark vessels used to give life to
diabolic Neanderthal homo-sapiens!

It started with aboriginal people migrating from Africa before
they were exiled from their lands...

Now in November we feast and give thanks to one of the
greatest slaughters done by white man!

Kill, steal, destroy and play the victim is their motto while
camouflaged as good Christian neighbors…

The Senegal of Satan has stolen our inheritance disguised as
Jews and sent us to suffer slave labor!

History is whited out while religion is whitewashed and
replaced with paganism and white idols…

Hollywood gave us their version of a third world mix of races
under the rulership of white power!

We have adopted pagan ways and their God while forfeiting
on the promise, we made our Father…

We have accepted their lies and allowed them to write us out
of the book that only has one author!

I live 4 God, put faith in God & my love for God is why I
spread the truth to all who listen…

I know Yeshua by only one name and it's not Jesus Christ
therefore I am not a Christian!

CHAPTER 7

BLOOD BROTHERS

According to the apocalyptic Book of Enoch, the Watchers were fallen angelic beings, described as both the sons of God and the sons of heaven who were assigned to watch over humans. It's understood that the women's beauty on earth was

so great that they caught the attention of the watchers. This beauty led the watchers to abandon the role as the watchers of humans to being consort to the women on earth.

Gen 6:1-4

When man began to multiply in the land daughters were born to them, the sons of God saw the daughters of man were attractive; so, they took as their wives any they chose. Then the Lord said, 'My Spirit shall not abide in man forever for he is flesh so his days shall be a 120 years. When the sons of God came into the daughters of man, they bore children to them called Nephilim. These were the mighty men who were of old, the men of renown.

These Nephilim's were preferred to as demigods as well; I will explain using scriptures, the book of Enoch and the Torah along with logic.

The scripture Genesis 6:1-4 is sandwiched between the birth of Noah and the flood. The position of this passage prompted 1 Enoch and Genesis Apocryphon to question whether Lamech was Noah's father or whether Noah was a demigod.

The ancient world is full of myths about demi-gods, the product of the love or lust of a god or goddess for a human being. The idea of a divine fathering is not as foreign to the Bible. The story in **Genesis 18 and Genesis 21** implies that Yahweh, or one of his messengers, impregnated Sarah. Eve's statement that she created Cain with the Lord in **Genesis4:1** and the story about the angel's visit to Manoah's wife also imply conception through a divine father in **Judges 13:2-25**.

Biblical stories avoid the kind of mythological details found in ancient Near Eastern and Greco-Roman accounts of the birth of demi-gods. Importantly none of these biblical accounts adds lust to divine beings, and only Samson inherits superhuman powers and behaves like a demigod. The closest we have in the Bible to the ancient Near Eastern and Greco-Roman accounts of a divine being feeling lust for human women, taking them, and producing demigods, is in a brief scripture found in Genesis 6, immediately preceding the flood story.

 It seems that ancient Israelites had much more to say about these demigods, but this material was lost or suppressed by ones responsible for composing the bible. Monotheistic religion does not easily connect to the idea of demigods, since this not only anthropomorphizes God, but also speaks about lesser gods. Later bible scholars switched the lesser gods to angels. The meaning of 'children of Elohim' could be literal Elohim's offspring or just a term for divinities or gods. Early interpreters, however, started calling these beings angels or messengers of God and not "gods" themselves. The word angel in Greek means messenger and in Hebrew it means "to send." Once it became accepted in Judaism that other gods do not exist, which became the standard belief. After a while these heavenly beings were demoted to the status of just lower beings created by god.

In 1 Enoch, Lamech, the father of Noah, reacts with panic upon seeing his new son's appearance:**1 Enoch 106:2-5**

Noah's body was white as snow and red like a flower of a rose, the hair on his head was white like wool, his eyes were beautiful; and when he opened his eyes, he made the whole house bright like the sun. When he was taken from the hand of the midwife, he opened his mouth and spoke to the Lord of righteousness. His father Lamech was afraid of him and fled, he went to his father Methuselah, and he said to him: "I have begotten a strange son; he is not like a man but like the children of the angels of heaven, of a very different type, and not like us.

The story continued with Methuselah going to his father Enoch consulting about this strange child. Enoch calms Methuselah and Lamech down, explaining that Noah's fantastic appearance is connected to the role he will play in history. This story's account of the way Noah's father reacted is firsthand proof that demigods or angelic beings mated with humans and had kids that appeared white in color.

God decided to create two distinct nations and races. The white man was not a completely new creation, Something similar had happened before in history where all the people were black but white-looking people popped up here and there, and at that time it was considered a mere curse in the form of leprosy, albinism, or off springs from angelic beings. Later God decided to make such a people out of the womb of a black woman; therefore, a white nation was officially birthed. This particular white man wasn't exactly an albino, he wasn't a leper either, this wasn't a spiritual curse or a medical condition, he was actually to be that way naturally. This theory has been argued throughout history by many religious scholars implying the archangel Samuel from the garden of Eden, who begot Cain may have impregnated Rebekah also. They're implicating Samuel is Esau's real father and also the angel that Jacob may have wrestled with. However, let us continue exploring all logical angles till we discover a portion of the truth in biblical text. This historical event was recorded in the bible in Genesis starting from chapter24. The Old Testament is an accurate historical book, supported by other historical texts.

The origin of a white race first began with black women and continued through a black woman called Rebekah. After years of failing to conceive, God finally open Rebekah's womb after her husband Isaac prayed for her, and lo and behold, she conceived twins. The twin pregnancy troubled her, and she asked God what on earth was happening inside her womb. She was clearly told by God that she is carrying two different nations (races) in her womb.

When the boys was born, only the color and race of the firstborn twin is described because he was the one who was born different. There was no need to describe the second-born twin because he was normal, he looked just like his mother and father, and every other human of that time, he had brown skin. Genesis says the firstborn twin was born RED and hairy, so he was named Esau, which means hairy. The normal-looking second-born twin came out holding his brother's heel, trying to push his older brother back inside their mother's womb, so he was named Jacob, which means deceptive. However, God favored and loved the deceptive boy more than his older brother Esau, so when Jacob was grown, God changed his name to Israel, he was to be the father of God's chosen nation.

Esau on the other hand was the first white/red human being on this earth was like a cursed child because God did not love him. His behavior throughout was problematic, he was the slow twin so growing up Jacob had an upper hand over him because Jacob was cunning. Esau sold his birthright to his clever little brother for a bowl of soup, fulfilling the prophecy told to Rebekah when she was pregnant, that the older will be a servant of the younger brother. Needless to say, as stupid as Esau was, his father Isaac loved him more; he was considered his favored son. Rebekah knew Jacob was the one chosen by God, so she made sure Jacob got all the blessings and this is when enmity between the blood brothers was born. Esau hated Jacob and sought to kill him.

The blessing Jacob received was actually from God because he was the chosen one, **Genesis 27:27-29**. Part of Jacob's blessing was that all people and nations should bow to him and serve him, but not only all peoples and nations, but that Esau his own older brother will be his servant as the scripture foretold 'The older shall serve the younger.' '**Genesis 25:23.**

Esau was favored by his father although through deception Jacob got the original blessing, Esau through tears begged his Father for a blessing too and Isaac out of the love and sympathy he had for his first-born, he gave Esau a temporary blessing.

However, because of Israel continued disobedience towards their God, God took the blessing from them and temporarily gave it to Jacob's rival Esau. King Solomon, a descendant of Jacob and manifestation of the supremacy over all nations, all Kings of the world bowed down to King Solomon. But because of his disobedience, Solomon was told by God that his blessing would be given to his servant, Esau and that was the beginning of the rise of Edom, or rather white people. That is why Esau/Edom or white people as we call them today are enjoying the temporary blessing of having all peoples and nations on earth bow down including Jacob. Jacob is supposed to be the race/nation over the whole earth, but this blessing was taken away from him, **(Jacob's trouble)** as the bible calls it.

Esau took wives from Africans/Canaanites but his attraction to Pagan Africans/ Canaanites grieved his God-fearing mother and father so much. According to history, and Jewish texts, Esau's two Canaanite wives, Adah and Aholibamah were pagan whores. They dwelt in Esau's tent but at night went back to their people and prostituted themselves. Because these two wives were such a thorn in the flesh of his mother Rebekah, he then decided to take on a third wife, a daughter of Ishmael, Bashemath, to please his parents. But according to history, his third wife was worse than Canaanites because through union with Bashemath he conspired with his uncle Ishmael to kill

Isaac and Jacob and eliminate the seed of Israel and replace it with his people therefore today the Edomites born from the womb of Ishmael's daughter Bashemath are what we know today as the Jews.

Just like the Israelites or Hebrews came from four black women, through the seed of Jacob, Leah, Rachel, Bilhah, and Zilpah. The Edomites, or white people also came from the wombs of three different pagan women, all black as well, Adah, Aholibamah and Bashemath. That is why scientifically, there is no denying white people originated from Africans because their white father had to impregnate black women for them to be born.

I believe Esau seeds were more like him than their mothers. It was the purpose of God to birth a completely new race. When a white man has a baby with a black woman, the baby come out more white than black as they grow up. Esau's descendants by three black women were born white, and as the generations pro-created they became whiter and whiter.

Now, while Jacob and his 4 wives were foreigners, travelers, and never quite settling in their own land, Esau on the other hand, through his temporary blessing was smart enough to travel to a new country and dwell in the mountains and establish empires and kingdoms. Esau's descendants had Kings before Israel had their first King, Saul. Esau quickly became more advanced and powerful than his brother. Esau was even richer than Jacob when they met years later after they had initially fallen out. When Esau heard that his little brother was running away from their uncle Laban, he went to meet him, and Esau had a company of 400 men, whilst Jacob only had his 4 wives and numerous children. This proves within a short time; Esau had established himself as some sort of Lord/Chief/King over the peoples of the land while his brother Jacob was actually homeless.

So, when the Babylonians came to destroy the temple centuries later, in what was the ultimate fall of Jacob, it was Esau who quickly took advantage of that fall and took over; joined forces with the Roman Empire, and helped chase away the remnant of Israel, who fled into Africa in which was the end of them being a nation. The Roman elite converted the Ottoman Turks and fellow Edomites to Judaism, replacing the vast black Jews.

Esau had become so advanced that even when Yeshua was born, the King of that era was Herod, a white Edomite who ruled over the remnant of black Jews in the Middle East, therefore Yeshua referred to them as the lost sheep of Israel. They were truly lost not just spiritually but they had no identity as well. It was so bad that the black Jews had to work for the Roman Empire, (the tax collectors).

The black Jews were in political bondage and oppression from white rule, so they were anticipating the birth of a black Jew Messiah, whom they believed would come and free them from bondage and be their earthly King. But when Yeshua came, he was a poor carpenter's son so most doubted him, because he was nothing like the glorious King they thought had been prophesied. Even John the Baptist was like, 'Who are you, are you even the one?' Yeshua didn't physically free the black Jews, instead their suffering under the Roman Empire continued.

Edom ruled along with the Roman Empire, their power and influence financed the transatlantic slave trade. Esau and his descendants became the superior race over all humanity and in the name of racism committed inhumane atrocities. The book of Obadiah explains in detail the fate of Edom, and how Esau and his seeds will eventually pay for their sins and atrocities against humanity but especially against his brother Jacob, the chosen one, to whom he is a servant.

JEW-NOT

Judgement has arrived for the Senegal of liars to repay
reparations for stealing our birthrights...

The bloodline of Shem extends to the negro Hebrews which is
identified as the black Israelites!

Anti-Semitic is a cover-up used to disguise & conceal the truth
from being exposed to the public...

Khazars migrated from a Europe Turkic tribe to Israel &
formed a democratic elite called republic!

We moved Father to anger and caused his wrath to reign down
upon us as a generational curse...

The Jew-not gentiles financed slave trading to rid themselves
of the Semitic people God chose first!

The Khazars extended their reach from Israel to every corner
of the globe as a one world order...

Their Illuminati movement has been the main power source
for controlling the America borders!

The United Kingdoms and States of Babylon is scheduled to
fall once the spiritual veil has drop...

So, all Khazar vamps exposed to the light will lose their false
Jewish claim so call them Jew-not!

Hebrews have awaken from a 400 plus year slumber and
stripped away the chains of brainwashing...

I am no longer your African American slave because I can
now breathe by using truth as my oxygen!

WHITE PRIDE

Like a trojan horse trampling over nations changing history,
religious tampering, and rewriting law…

One womb shall bare 2 seeds called Jacob who I love and the
other whom I do not love called Esau!

Yet without love he shall grow stronger than him whom I
chose and become the mightiest of nations…

This ungodly breed shall mingle his seeds with gentiles and
become spoiled by my sons of damnation!

From the bloodline of Edomites shall come kings bringing
death, destruction, and worldwide genocide…

As they destroy empires and lay waste to other nations making
the eagle their symbol of white pride!

Their reign of terror shall be endless upon the seeds of Jacob
with no mercy shown to their enemy…

Their false doctrine shall brainwash my children in accepting
paganism to erase their memory of me!

Robbed of their true inheritance and taught to hate their
brother but love their spiteful neighbor...

The Senegal of Satan will move to the land I promised
Abraham and pretend to be the ones I favor!

They will fertilize lands with my disobedient children blood
and claim themselves heir to my throne...

But the heaven they have made on earth shall become hell
when I decide to bring my children home!

From Isaac's bloodline came the messiah Yeshua my beloved
son whom I allowed to be crucified...

For on judgement day rulers shall replace servants as gentiles
humbly serve Israel with white pride!

I will not forgive their trespasses, nor will I forgive the false
image that bears a false name of my son...

You can white out the whole world, but I am God, and I will
cast a shadow that outshines the sun!

CHAPTER 8

LUCIFER

We've been taught for many centuries that Lucifer was once an angel created by God before becoming Satan, the wicked devil out to destroy humanity. He's known as commander and chief of demons living in hell plotting mankind's downfall, also planning to return to heaven and take the holy throne from the Most High. We know the stories, but do we know whether it's true or false?

The name lucifer appears one time in the bible in **Isaiah 14:12**. 'How you fall from heaven, O Lucifer, son of the morning; How are you cut to the ground; you who weakened the nations!'. Many people for centuries have equated this Lucifer with Satan, the devil.

There are two passages in the Old Testament that are frequently used to teach Satan's a fallen angel. The two passages are: 1) **Isaiah 14:12-15**, a taunt against the king of Babylon. **2) Ezekiel 28:11-19**, a lament about the king of Tyre. Satan isn't named in either passage therefore we shouldn't make claims that they are describing Satan. These text have different opinions, rather than direct observation. Both passages is written in poetry using vivid picture language and imagery typically used by the OT prophets.

Religious leaders teach about the fall of Satan, stating that Satan was once a beautiful angel, the greatest of all created beings. He rebelled against God becoming a devil before man was created. Originally, it were only three archangels, Michael, Gabriel, and Lucifer; each ruled one third of the angels. Michael and Gabriel remained faithful to God, but Satan rebelled, taking one third of the angels with him, who became the demonic forces.

Some teaches Satan was the heavenly choirmaster with musical instruments built into his body. This presumption is supported in **Ezekiel 28:13**:

"the workmanship of thy tabrets and of thy pipes was prepared in thee in the day that thou was created".

This translation is only found in the King James Version. Some teach there was even a population of humans on the earth before Adam, known as a pre-adamic race. Lucifer was given authority over them before they rebelled and was judged by a flood. Then Lucifer became Satan and after judgement, the earth was remade as described in Genesis chapters 1 and 2. This is part of the 'gap theory', an attempt to combine Genesis account with the theory of evolution, by saying there was a long gap in time between the first two verses in Genesis.

Two other scriptures are used to support this teaching. The 1st is **Luke 10:17** when they said, 'Lord, in your name even the demons submit to us!' **Luke 10:18**, He (Yeshua) said to the seventy sent out into the harvest-field, 'I watched Satan fall from heaven like a flash of lightning but when studied this does not refer to a fall of Satan but the effect the mission of the seventy had on the powers of darkness.

Let's discuss **Revelation 12:1-12** when John sees a vision of the great red dragon identified as, that ancient serpent who is called the devil, and Satan. Michael along with his angels fought Satan, the deceiver of the whole world, who was thrown down to earth and his angels with him. This event is indicated in **Revelations 12:10** when the loud voice in heaven says: 'now have come the salvation and the power and the kingdom of our God and the authority of his Messiah, for the accuser of our brothers has been thrown down.' This did not happen at the beginning of time, but at Yeshua's cross where he brought salvation, demonstrated the power of the kingdom, and defeated the enemy. Yeshua made a similar statement before his death in **John 12:31** Now is the time for judgment on this world; now the prince of this world will be driven out. And I, when I am lifted up from the earth, will draw all people to myself.

It's questionable whether Luke 10 or the Revelation 12 passage describes the fall of Satan from heaven before the beginning of time, but its apparent both describe the defeat of Satan achieved by the ministry, death, and resurrection of Yeshua.

There's references to fallen angels in Jude 6 and 2 Peter 2:4 but no indication is given that Satan was associated with them or that he fell at the same time. These passages are probably referring to the mysterious account of the time when the sons of God lusted after the daughters of men **(Gen 6:1-4).** Both Peter and Jude uses this event as warnings about false teachers. There is no passages in the Bible which give a clear and unambiguous teaching about the origin of Satan, or a fall of Satan from a place of glory.

Isaiah use Lucifer as a name for the king of Babylon who had set himself among the gods. Babylonian worship was strongly based on astrology, but the Babylonians and Assyrians personified the morning star Venus as Ishtar. The message of Isaiah is that none of the Babylonian gods are able to save the king, as all gods are powerless before the One True God. In the Ancient Near East, it's common practice for kings to believe they were incarnations of gods. So, when a king was defeated in battle and his city was captured it was a sign that their god had also been defeated by more powerful gods of the victorious enemy. The enemy would tear down images of the god and take them captive, placing them in the temple of their own god to demonstrate its superior power. This would explain why the Philistines placed the captured ark of the covenant in the temple of their god Dagon.

The king of Tyre is described as the signet of perfection; full of wisdom and perfect in beauty in **Ezekiel 28:12**. Many say Satan can only be this not a king or city. However, in the same oracles against Tyre, it claimed this for itself: **Ezekiel 27:3** Tyre, you have said, 'I am perfect in beauty.' **Ezekiel 28:2** 'Your heart is proud, and you said, 'I am a god.' The prince of Tyre's wisdom, trade and wealth are described in Ezekiel 28:4-5. The prince of Tyre compared his mind with the mind of a god in **Ezekiel 28:6**.

Two distinguished scriptures used to support the view that Satan is indeed a fallen angel is when Yeshua told the Pharisees, 'You are from your father the devil; He was a murderer from the beginning and does not stand in the truth' written in **John 8:44**. From the beginning means for all the time he has existed. Also, in John's first letter 1 John 3:8, 'Everyone who commits sin is a child of the devil because the devil has been sinning from the beginning.' These passages would indicate that the devil has always been a sinner and a murderer, and that he has no great and beautiful past.

It causes philosophical problems on a level whether something that was created evil and something that was created good and became evil. The significant matter is we do know Satan which in Hebrew means adversary does exists but what we don't know is his true identity. This is a question not asked nor answered in the Bible. Did the most high God El create Satan as an adversary or is he one of his 70 children? Satan's existence has definitely been used for decades by religious leaders to test believers faith. Preachers have taught us it's not God's will that we sin, but it is God's will we are tested and tempted. Consistently through the New Testament it is taught that testing is part of the Christian walk written in **James 1:2-4;** so, we learn patience, strengthen our faith, and prove our love for God. Therefore, our love for God is a positive response and choice. So, to choose to love God, it is necessary to have opposite influence to choose to reject. Also using logic and scripture we can uncover the truth

FALLING STAR

From a righteous position in Heaven amongst glory and grace
with a prodigious lavish shine...

Father's most beautiful creation possessed beauty but lacked
obedience for Elohim the divine!

Distraught with jealousy in a fit of rage he waged war against
Father the creator of all creation...

Beaten, battered, bruised, and stripped of glory with foolish
pride to blame for his elimination!

He was no match for the arch angel Michael in a battle for the
high throne of Elohim the supreme...

The prince of light is now the prince of darkness for it is
written there can only be one king of kings!

Thrown from heaven to dwell beneath the earth now known as
the fallen star without his shine...

Till he influenced the elite to discover Microsoft technology to
control and alter the human mind!

He speaks to us through televised media giving us false
information to distract us from the truth...

He feed upon our wicked desires, our greed for power and our
misguiding probes of finding proof!

Clones have replaced people and demons trick spirits to loan
their bodies in exchange for favors...

Computerized spies keeps a watch on the world through
iPhones and electronic communications!

We are the light for this falling star by being the main power
source that allows him to shine…

So, we must expose illuminati's plot by showing the devil he
cannot and will not control mankind!

CHAPTER 9

REVELATIONS OF YAHWEH

The truth has always been hidden in plain sight yet we continue to be spiritual blind to it. Heaven has provided me a window so I may see beyond the clouds of lies. My discoveries come from the bible so I will use scriptures to expose what many have overlooked for centuries.

I found two stories about creation of two different accounts from two different deities. The first story tell of a God name El written Elohim in the bible which in Hebrew is plural for Gods. The first account in **Genesis 1:26** states 'Let us make man and woman in our image and our likeness.' As we know the deity El is depicted as a 'he' which is a masculine image. So, if man is made in the image of El then what feminine image is woman made in? Spiritual scholars have attempted to answer this question by saying God is male and female. If that truly was the case then humanity would have male and female parts making them hermaphrodites; but Unfortunately, that's not the case because males and females are separate creations.

The bible has given us the historical proof we need to determine that a Mother Goddess was present during creation and her name was Asherah, wife of El the most high God. At one time this Mother Goddess was actually worshipped and highly celebrated by cakes being baked for her, incense burned to her, and drinks poured out to her. '**Jeremiah**' **7:18** The children gather wood, the fathers kindle fire, and the women knead dough to bake for the Queen of heaven. '**Jeremiah 44:17** We will burn incense to the Queen of Heaven and will pour out drink offerings to her just as we and our fathers, our kings and our officials done in the towns of Judah and in the streets of Jerusalem'. Even King David and his son King Solomon worshipped her. Biblical scriptures also reveal at one time Asherah was acknowledged, worshipped, and highly celebrated alongside El.

El and Asherah created Adam and Lilith in what is known as the first creation of man and woman. In the garden Adam and Lilith was told by El to be fruitful and multiply with each other. No one really truly knows what happen inside the garden but the ones that was in the garden; however, we can use common logic to speculate events that took place. Many biblical scholars like to say it was also a serpent lurking in the garden besides Adam and Lilith in which I find hard to believe. This serpent later came to be known as Satan by Christians. But if we use logic, we will first ask how did a deceitful animal symbolizing evil get in a garden made perfect by the most high God El? Next, we would ask how did this animal become associated with Satan when Satan first appearance is much later in the bible but in Hebrew, Satan mean Adversary. But logically someone did appear before Lilith in human form; seduced her, had sex with her and impregnated her. Although we're unable to determine what part Lilith played in this sexual encounter, we do know she left Adam in the garden and refused to return.

However, in (Greek) Apocalypse of **Baruch 3**, a biblical book excluded from the bible written by the scribe of Jeremiah name Baruch ben Neriah. This ancient book speaks about the garden of Eden and names Lilith's seducer as Samael an arch angel known as the lefthand of El. Samael is often described as a tempter of man, a seducer, and one who encourages and condones men to sin. In a sense, you might see him as a tester employed by God. Unlike traditional tales and ideas about Satan being the snake, this book explains that Samael rode the serpent as his mount and that the serpent doesn't appear to be an evil figure in disguise, but more so an extension of Samael or a creature he had directly manipulated.

Samael is also said to be the true father of Cain, implying that he was also able to seduce the second woman in the garden name Eve into another sexual encounter. The biblical book (3Baruch) describes itself as a narrative by Baruch receiving a revelation from God concerning ineffable things that have always been pondered by man.

In this account, Baruch praises God daily and ask why he has allowed Jerusalem to suffer capture and Dominion under King Nebuchadnezzar, but he does not receive a response. Instead, God sends one of his angels to show Baruch the mysteries of the heavens, and in doing so, he hopes that Baruch will stop praying to him on this matter. Baruch agrees to this and is taken through the layers of heaven by the angel, each of which Baruch describes in great detail. By the time they reached the third layer, Baruch asks the angel to show him the tree that led Adam astray, and the angel speaks these words in **3 Baruch 4:8-9**

'It is the vine, which the angel Samael planted, whereat the Lord was angry, and he cursed him and his plant, while also on this account God didn't permit Adam to touch it, therefore Samael being envious deceived Adam through this.

In this scripture account it shows the arch angel Samael was in the garden. Later it is foretold after Lilith leaves the garden, she becomes Samael's bride and together they have many kids in which one daughter in particular is named Lilim. She marries Cain who is her brother because they both share the same father, the arch angel Samael. In the second creation **Genesis 2:21-25** we are introduced to Eve who also like Lilith were seduced by the arch angel Samael and bore twins by 2 different fathers. A child name Cain was conceived from Samael and a child name Abel conceived from Adam.

Genesis 4:1

'And Adam had relations with his wife Eve, and she conceived and gave birth to Cain. With the help of the Lord, I have brought forth a man, she said. Later she gave birth to Cain's brother Abel.'

This deceptional pregnancy got Adam and Eve expelled from the garden of Eden. God spoke these words to Samael.

Genesis 3:15

'I will put enmity between you and the woman, and between your offspring and hers; They will strike at your head, while you strike at their heel.'

Cain is known throughout history for killing his brother Abel in an act of jealous and envy, but it did not go unpunished. God forced Cain to leave the garden giving him a sign so that anyone who met Cain could not harm him. Cain and his wife started a family, founded a city, and named it Enoch after their son.

When studying biblical scriptures you must avoid the traditional teachings you have been taught and examine each scripture with new eyes; for the truth is hidden in plain sight.

It is said that El and Asherah had 70 children together in which this bible scripture details this council of Gods.

Deuteronomy 32:8-9 '"When the Most High God El gave the nations as inheritances he separated the sons of man and set the boundaries of the peoples according to his number of sons. For Yahweh's portion was his people; Jacob was the lot of his inheritance.'

The scripture above was worded different from the Dead Sea scroll scripture but both have the same meaning; In the dead sea scroll passage the sky god El, also called the Heavenly Father or El Elohim (meaning "most High of all the gods") El divided all humans into 70 nations and gave the nation of Israel to his son Yahweh. These scriptures speak consistent with different gods ruling different geographical areas like kings in the ancient near east religions. Also see the reference in the Bible to the 70 nations emerging after the Flood in **Exodus 15:11**. Also the praise the children of Israel sings there mentions other gods 'Who is like unto thee, O LORD, among the gods? Who is like thee, glorious in holiness, Fearful in praises, doing wonders?' During this precise time the son of El name Yahweh claimed his inheritance which is Israel and identified himself to Moses. Yahweh was sometime called Lord by the children of Israel.

Psalms 82 This scripture is self-explanatory if you're reading it with an uncontaminated mind because it clearly expresses one God's anger toward the other gods. It starts out by saying:

'God presides in the great assembly and renders judgment among the gods: How long will you defend the unjust and show partiality to the wicked?

The gods know nothing, so they understand nothing. They walk about in darkness; all the foundations of the earth are shaken.

I said, 'You are "gods"; you are all sons of the Most High. But you will die like mere mortals; you will fall like every other ruler.

Rise up, O God, judge the earth, for all the nations are your inheritance.'

In the beginning El was very much present in the scriptures as creator of Heaven and Earth; known to be a loving and merciful Most High God.

Overtime El the Father God was replaced by his son Yahweh, the revengeful and jealous war god. Yahweh was on a mission to become the one and only god by usurping his siblings, erasing his mother Asherah from history, and exacting himself as the most high Father God.

In time people began to merge Yahweh with his Father El while pairing him as husband to Asherah instead of son. His siblings were considered false gods making Yahweh the only true god.

94

A shift in authority began with this complete takeover, exalting Yahweh's name above any and all others to be worship by every nation. The bible proves that this war type god was a completely different God from the beginning that spoke with Abraham and Jacob.

The children of Israel over a period of time became to be a feared nation protected by a feared god name Yahweh. This conquering god took no prisoners as he led the Israelites to the land promised to Abraham descendants by the Father God El. The conquering god Yahweh protected his inheritance by any means even if it meant killing man, woman, and child.

1 Samuel 15:2-3

This is what the god Yahweh says: 'I will punish the Amalekites for what they did to Israel when they ambushed them as they came up from Egypt. Now go, attack the Amalekites, and totally destroy all that belongs to them. Do not spare them; put to death men and women, children and infants, cattle and sheep, camels, and donkeys.'

Over time we were taught it was only one merciful loving God with a wicked nemesis that wanted nothing more than to sit on his father's throne. This archenemy was called by many names like Lucifer, Satan, devil, prince of darkness, ancient serpent, and great dragon. However, if we use logic along with scripture, we may be able to see a portion of the truth. Therefore, I ask you to continue reading without the prejudice of tradition and focus more on the scriptural proof.

Yahweh clearly commanded in **Exodus 20:4**: "You shall not make for yourself any carved image, or any likeness of anything that is in heaven above, or that is in the earth beneath." Yet here Moses is instructed by Yahweh to make two cherubim of gold of hammered work. If making images of any heavenly object is wrong, then why did Yahweh command Moses to make some on the ark of the covenant?

In **Numbers 21:8** during their long journey to the land of Edom; the Israelites struggled with hunger and dehydration in the wilderness and so they complained to Yahweh. But the Israelite god was annoyed by their grumbling and sent forth a rain of fiery serpents, revealed to have been the Seraphim themselves who conjured serpents of fire, that bit the people thereby killing many of them. In the mist of desperation, the survivors begged the prophet Moses to pray to Yahweh and end their torment to which Moses obliged. Yahweh told Moses to craft a fiery serpent made of copper and set it on a pole, whereby those who look upon and worship the idol will not succumb to death once they are bitten by the snakes. When Yahweh ordered Moses to create an idol it involved the crafting of a serpent made of copper intertwined around a wooden pole. This idol is known as Nehushtan, this image could imply that the idol was a likeness of his own.

In ancient Israel Yahweh was seen with many draconic features and these features in general have even been described in many verses throughout the Old Testament. One example is Yahweh explains that a fire is kindled within his nostrils that will burn through the lowest Hell and it shall consume the Earth with its increase and set ablaze the foundations of the mountains. In **Psalms 18:8**, it describes Yahweh as having smoke going up from his nostrils and devouring fire from out of his mouth.

Yahweh is painted as a vengeful, divine warrior who more often than not violently annihilates his enemies. More than that, the Hebrew Bible uses specific imageries repeatedly to describe his physical presence on Earth leaving us with an undeniable image of none other than an incredibly powerful dragon. The imagery of Yahweh assuming the form of a divine dragon is interesting given that dragons or serpents in general were often regarded as enemies in biblical tales.

This explain why he required a massive portable tent known as a Tabernacle as was recorded in Exodus. For 440 years, this building-sized tent was the earthly dwelling of Yahweh, where offerings of prepared meals as well as sacrificed livestock were given on a daily basis, and a thick smoke was known to appear at the door when it was opened. However, this was far from the only instance that Yahweh accepted edible offerings.

In the Book of **Numbers 31** Yahweh commands the prophet Moses and his army of 12,000 men to take revenge against the Midianites: and to wage war on their people. After murdering every Midianite man and their leaders, pillaging their city, and capturing all the women and children, Moses commands his troops to kill all those who have had intercourse. Afterwards, Moses and his men divide their plunder and give a portion of it to Yahweh, which includes 32 Midianite virgins who were never heard from again. Moses and Eleazar the priest received the gold from all the military commanders, all kinds of jewelry and crafted objects, and were given to Yahweh as a gift. It is believed that the reason why Yahweh prefers virgin females is because pure untainted blood of a virgin woman is implicated as a delicacy for a dragon.

The Bible describes Yahweh as the one true God who delivered Israel from Egypt and gave the Ten Commandments, Then God spoke all these words. Unlike the common descriptions of God, Yahweh is depicted to Israel as a jealous and vengeful God who would not permit His people to make idols or follow gods of other nations or worship gods known by other names. Yahweh demanded the role of the one true God in the hearts and minds of Israel to the point where he even had the Israelites craft an idol for him and more than just permit the idol, he essentially forces the Israelites to make and worship it by threatening their lives.

Yahweh has even garnered the Gnostics to make and worship a similar deity known as the Demiurge. The likely reason why Yahweh is depicted as such is possibly due to the fact that this is the same God who incited the War in Heaven, caused his mother Asherah's leave of absence, and caused an emotional toll on his Father El. The tyranny of Yahweh caused his Father El to send Yeshua as ransom to retake the inherence given to his unmerciful son Yahweh. Yeshua and El conspired a plan to deceive Yahweh after realizing and seeing his true motive was to become supreme god over his, father, mother, and siblings.

Yeshua is worldly known as Jesus was born through a virgin so he may become flesh. His mission was to be the human sacrifice so we may be exonerated from under the tyranny of Yahweh the god of this world. While dwelling as flesh walking amongst humanity. It was also Yeshua's mission to teach us about our Father we have forgotten, El the most high supreme God of creation. Yeshua reminded us that our father loved us, and he taught faith and peace rather than death and destruction. Before his earthly death Yeshua made a promise before ascending into heaven that he would return to lead us back to the land promised by El; breaking the punishment of slavery inflicted upon the Israelites by Yahweh.

Till Yeshua returns our land is occupied by the seed of the arch angel Samael from the garden of Eden. Samael seeds mixed with Esau's seeds trample the land calling themselves Jews claiming to be from the tribe of Juda which are lies.

Revelations 2:9

'I know thy tribulation, and thy poverty (but thou art rich), and the blasphemy of them that say they are Jews, and they are not, but are a synagogue of Satan.'

Satan means adversary in Hebrew which is one of the names Samael was called.

FATHER'S LIGHT

One day the king of kings in the high blue skies decided it was
time to extend his eternal family...

So, Father of light spoke heaven and earth into existence from
nothing but these commandments!

In this dark universal void Father said, 'let there be light' and
so it was divided between day and night...

Next, he called upon firmament to separate the waters from
the heavenly skies so fertilized soil could interact with light!

Then he created the children of heaven to twinkle and shine
like the rays of the sun and the glow of the moon...

But one star felt he should shine the brightest and allowed
envy to weaken his heart from the pride it consumed!

Yet Father ignored the signs and continued to flood the earth
with many different forms of species...

But it was when he created man the morning star felt
neglected and rebelled challenging Father's thesis!

Vanity and ambition took the place of devotion, so a battle
ensued causing the star to lose his shine...

Thrown from the high heaven to reign for eternity in darkness
for his jealousy rage toward mankind!

Defeated yet determined to prove humanity was not worthy of
existence as Father's prized creation...

So, the fallen star manipulated wicked hearts and brilliant
minds of the world by advancing civilization!

Self-proclaimed purifying males used their dominated
egotistic pride to alter verses in the biblical Canon…

But the Hebrew lamp of God came to testify of a great light
that sent his final word as a sacrifice for humanity!

So, as we broaden our spiritual minds to resist the poison lies
told to deceive us and keep us in the dark…

May my Father's Light shine upon the world to guide us back
to the truth that speaks silently in our hearts!

SCRIBE OF GOD

Illuminati declared war on God's people with covid-19 as their
mass destructive take over...

I was given wings of a Phoenix to fly from the ashes once this
corrupt world is given a make-over!

I am a prince to the king of kings therefore my prodigal birth
makes me an enemy to death...

I wasn't born with no silver spoon because my life outvalues
the price of commonwealth!

Once I turn on the faucet of revenge for whoever pierced my
side releasing a never-ending flow.

I shall avenge my death by allowing my brother to enter when
he stands knocking at the door!

With hair like wool and eyes like a fiery flame I bear close
resemblance to the chosen son...

With complexion like burnt brass I was given holy ink from
Father's pen to cut like a sharp tongue!

In my second death I was given the crown of life so I may
have an eternity to live again...

Time is not measured in years, months nor days and there is
absolutely no such thing as sin!

I write in parables to confuse the wicked and speak to the
purest of hearts and the sharpest minds...

Whatever God writes in Heaven he sends one of his angels to
whisper to me every single line!

I am his ancestor to the world, his poet to the misfortunate and the one he chose to be his scribe...

Yeshua wrote in sand what's written in heaven as I write the same words in hearts to inspire lives!

ADAM, LILITH, AND EVE

From the same dust we were created and given life beyond our
spiritual realm...

God said let us make man and woman in our image, so he
created her and him!

Born without sin but filled with grace from the creator of the
whole universe ...

We are the beginning of mankind and in thy book of life our
names are written first!

I have my Father's features given the name Adam recorded as
the first Hebrew man...

Emmanuel tells me I'm not along for I see Yeshua is with us
by his footprints in the sand!

How shall we multiply when we share the same dominance
and given the same assignment?

Whether you lay beneath me or beside me it's still our task to
replenish the environment!

Mythology has exposed your presence, yet scribes have
written you off as a demonic myth...

But Father said man should not be alone, so I was given Eve in
the place of my beloved Lilith!

Therefore, from the dust of the earth woman was recreated
from bone of my bone we reunited...

Let all who disagree with this poetic thesis speak but I'm not
the author I'm merely the writer!

God's words were transferred from stone to books including
and excluding many scriptures...

So, am I wrong to question the same history that whitewash
religion in books and motion pictures?

The cannon provides us with directions but it's up to us to
follow the trail of nonfiction and facts...

We may never truly know the story of Adam, Lilith, and Eve
but at least we know they black!

CROSS MY HEART

My thoughts forever wander so I close my eyes and allowed
my spirit to travel beyond this realm...

As I entered the gates of heaven, I'm greeted by the almighty
King of kings the Most High God Elohim!

Father what is the true meaning of the symbolic symbol that
has lived before Christianity was born?

'Does my son not say pick up your cross and follow him but
instead you fashioned yours to be worn!'

'You were led out of Africa in chains and now you wear them
with pride around your neck like a noose'...

'Your brain have been washed of knowledge of self and filled
with the harsh burdens deprived of truth!'

'Before my son was identified by man, he was known by no
other name but Yeshua the sacrificed lamb'...

'I am none other than God the Father of every nation my
descendent of Deuteronomy's curse, so I Am!'

'It was my son Constantine's goal to combine paganism with
Christianity calling it the crucifix of Christ'...

'Why worship a symbol for hatred and death then attach my
name when I'm the symbol for love and life?'

'Sunday is a pagan day meant for pagans to worship the sun
and yet my sabbath day you do not keep'...

'When I return, I will punish the shepherds who misled my
flock and redeem my bewildered misguided sheep!'

105

'You have ignored my covenant with your forefathers and crossed my heart by following your own desire'...

'As Marshall you were born again in the water and given the wings of a Phoenix baptized in holy fire!'

'So, inhale the smoke of God and allow your lungs to burst from the eternal flames of heavens furnace'...

'My Hebrew son give my people what I have given you and let them know judgement day is coming!'

CHAPTER 10

THE UNSPOKEN TRUTH

The truth always been in plain view but we have been mentally trained to ignore truth and believe the lie. The bible is a history book considered to be the written word of God, yet we allow others to interpret that truth for us. We give power and authority to preachers, pastors, and self-proclaimed prophets to tell, teach and explain the holy words of our creator. Most religious name-Sayers are literally steering you wrong on purpose by confusing you with false interpretations of the scriptures. In my complex uncontaminated mind, I will use those same scriptures to prove and steer you in the right direction.

The story of Noah has always been fascinating, intriguing, and unclear because certain key elements were missing whenever the story was told. The world was repopulated by 8 people, but do we really have a clue on who those 8 people were? The book of Enoch wasn't considered official scripture, but it was considered important and in fact it was so important they hid it amongst the Dead Sea scrolls found in Qumran. Let's examine the birth of Noah using scripture and logic.

Book of Enoch 105:1–3

"After time, my son Methuselah took a wife for his son Lamech, and she became pregnant by him. She brought forth a child, the flesh, which was as white as snow, and red as a rose; hair on his head was white like long wool; his eyes were beautiful. When he opened them, he illuminated all the house like the sun; the whole house abound with light. And when he was taken from the hand of the midwife and opened his mouth, he spoke to the Lord of righteousness. Lamech his father was afraid of him; and went to his own father Methuselah, and said, 'I have begotten a son unlike the other children. He is not human; but resembles the offspring of the angels of heaven. He is a different nature from us, altogether unlike us."

In these scriptures Lamech believed Noah was the son of a angel which clearly indicates angels were having children on earth. The color of the angel's children called Nephilim were white in which white skin was not common among humans at this time. Although Hollywood with their movies and other media outlets have shown Noah as a European Whiteman is completely false. Noah was described as having white skin, but we know that not only Europeans have white skin. Black people also can be born with white skin, and we refer to these people as albinos. Both of Noah's parents were black, a lineage traced all the way back to Adam, Lilith and Eve who was black despite the false teachings we been taught.

It's a proven scientific fact that white babies are not only born to Europeans. Black people can have white children, but white people cannot have a black child. Only way all races could exist on the planet is if they started dark and became lighter over time.

Enoch, Lamech, and Noah was all from the line of Seth (Adam's third son). So, if Noah was white and the other humans were not then they were likely brown or dark skinned. If the humans were brown or dark skinned, then it would've been passed down from Adam. If brown or dark skin was passed down from Adam, it would mean that Adam was most likely brown or dark skinned.

We are constantly bombarded with images of a white God and public images of Yeshua as a homosexual white man but why is that? If race doesn't matter and we are always told God is just a spirit without race, why is he always depicted as white and not the correct color; black? If Adam was made in the creator's image, then his creator too was black.

We must accept logic over tradition if we want to understand and unlock the mysteries of the bible. Let's examine the cursing of Canaan by Noah using scriptures and logic.

Gen 9:20 And Noah began to be a husbandman, and he planted a vineyard:

Gen 9:21 And he drank of the wine and was drunken; and he was uncovered within his tent.

Gen 9:22 And Ham, the father of Canaan, saw the nakedness of his father, and told his two brethren.

Gen 9:23 And Shem and Japheth took a garment and laid it upon their shoulders, went backward covering the nakedness of their father and with their faces backward they saw not their father's nakedness.

Gen 9:24 And Noah awoke from his wine and knew what his younger son had done unto him.

Gen 9:25 And he said, Cursed be Canaan; a servant of servants shall he be unto his brethren.

Gen 9:26 And he said, Blessed be the LORD God of Shem; and Canaan shall be his servant.

These scriptures brings to mind many un questions. Why would Noah curse a child for the sins of his father; doesn't the Bible condemn this in **Ezekiel 18:20**?

(The soul that sin shall die. The son shall not bear the sin of the father, neither shall the father bear the sin of the son).

Why didn't Noah not curse Ham? Why seeing your father naked a sin, after all, can a father not bathe in the same bath as his child? Why is Noah mad at this? What exactly did Ham do to

Noah? It is curious that Ham isn't linked with Canaan in verse 21 and then Canaan is cursed in verse 25. Ham, after all, had multiple children (4 boys at least which Canaan was presumably the youngest). Some might claim that Canaan was the most wicked child, but this is nowhere in this text. The bible never informs us about the individual name Canaan except the place of his decedent's residence and his lineage.

So why the nation of Canaan cursed? Moses, the same author of Genesis wrote **Lev 20:11**:

And the man that lieth with his father's wife hath uncovered his father's nakedness: both of them shall surely be put to death; their blood shall be upon them.

In this scripture we see nakedness is a euphemism for sexual relations so with these concepts in mind, Genesis 9 takes on a whole new meaning and becomes clear using logic:

Gen 9:20 Noah begins making wine

Gen 9:21 Noah gets drunk

Gen 9:22 Ham (father of Canaan) see his father is incapacitated makes advances on his mother. After all, sex is pleasurable, men tend to desire multiple partners, not many women are available after a global flood and his mother is probably still attractive due to pre-flood aging conditions. He gloats of his conquest to his brothers.

Gen 9:23 The brothers try damage control. They cover up their mother (is she drunk also?).

Gen 9:24 Noah comes back into consciousness and figures out that his wife is pregnant (after some time).

Gen 9:25-26 He curses the new nation that will be formed from this union.

The timelapse in verse 24 can be explained as a storyteller uses lapses in time. In Mat 3:13, Jesus appears, out of nowhere fully grown. The last time Mathew had talked about him, Jesus was just a child. Nowhere is there a development transition. It is normal to skip large segments of time in telling stories. In short, those who claim that Ham merely saw his father naked have no explanation. But logic and facts point to Canaan being the result of maybe an incestuous relationship between Noah's wife and Ham. Also, in the Book of Jasher it seems Ham may not have been Noah's wife Naamah's son because it only name Shem and Japheth as her children.

Book of Jasher, Chapter 5:14-18

And the Lord said to Noah, Take unto thee a wife, and beget children for I seen the righteous before me in this generation.

And thou shalt raise up a seed and thy children with thee in the midst of the earth; and Noah went and took a wife, and he chose Naamah the daughter of Enoch, and she was five hundred and eighty years old.

And Noah was four hundred and ninety-eight years old, when he took Naamah for a wife.

And Naamah conceived and bared a son, and his name was called Japheth, saying, God has enlarged me in the earth; and she conceived again and bared another son, and his name was called Shem, saying, God has made me a remnant, to raise up seed in the midst of the earth.

And Noah was five hundred and two years old when Naamah bared Shem, and the boys grew up and went in the ways of the Lord, in all that Methuselah and Noah their father taught them.

What is interesting about this scripture is what it does not say. What it doesn't say, is that Naamah was the mother of Ham. We can speculate that Noah possibly had another wife and that the result of his copulation with that wife was Ham.

111

YOU MADE A MONSTER OUT OF ME

I studied the holy Koran, Bible and Cepher in hopes to find the
truth hidden in the bowels of religion...

But all I discovered was cover-ups, lies & deception by the
synagogue to white-out their competition!

Life's a bitch but I'm trying to make it with her till I die & she
moves on to the next poor unlucky soul...

You took what should never been taken now you attempt to
return what should have never been stole!

I been running from hell hounds leaving fire trails of burnt
footprints and the aroma from torched flesh...

You made a monster out of me, and I became a living
breathing curse that God saw fit to still bless!

I wrestled with Satan and won but the battle scars remain on
my spirit making me a walking crucifix...

I fucked illuminati by cheating death, but I will always cherish
and love life even though life's a bitch!

You threw dirt on me and still couldn't cover up my shine
because my light is too bright to conceal....

It's not the crown on my head but the crown in my heart that
makes my kingship and kingdom real!

I'm drowning in betrayal please throw me an anchor of loyalty
& save me from suffocation by treason...

I'll be that monster you been wanting with ice water in my
veins so I can survive player hating season!

This is the story of the monster you created, the creature you crossed out and the beast you made me…

So, take a look at America's illegitimate baby & all the hate I have to give cause it's the hate you gave me!

THE DAY OF TRUTH

Hate may misguide our steps in life, but death can never walk
in my Father footprints....

Whomsoever bears the blame for 9/11 will surely face the
supreme ruler over all governments!

My tears mixed with their innocent blood outvalues oil,
economics, politics, and power...

It was man, greed and hate but not religion that guided those
planes into our towers!

I pledge allegiance to Yeshua and honor only God under the
flag of humanity...

I discovered the page ripped from the book of revelations and
it read a war has been declared on Christianity!

Thousands of lives lost and trillions in repairs as the whole
world watched in horror and shock...

Mass destruction signifies the end of time but only Father
know the final hour the clock will stop!

Their screams will echo for years to come but never can we
silence the cries of hope....

The media tells their story, my poetry tells mine and 9/11 is
the unedited version of both!

Only God knows the truth that is buried beneath government
cover ups, politics and lies...

You may blind the world with liberty and justice, but nothing
gets pass my Father eyes!

So, give me truth or give me death to a county that is built
from blood, war, and slave labor...

Was 9/11 an act of terrorist or Bush sacrificing 2,996 lives to
incite war with our Muslim neighbors?

The day of truth will come under the stars of heaven along
with judgment for the stripes on our savior's back...

Once we see past all the smoke on 9/11 then maybe we can get
a clear picture of the explosive facts!

BAPHOMET TRUTH

Smile now cry later but your goat head statue can never
replace the shepherd leading God's flock...

Your satanic scriptures are written with deceit to teach
separation and discredit prophets like Enoch!

Lucien Greaves and Malcolm Jarry founded the temple of lies
decorated with symbols of a pentagram...

The lion of Judah are the true sheep of God that will be
restored by the blood of the sacrificed ram!

I am one of many messengers for the most high sent to speak
truth about the works of my divine Father ...

I testify to illuminati's false allegations by using my pen as a
sword to cut down their one world order!

Government scandals to slander and defame whoever speaks
out against their egotistic plots and rules...

I hereby challenge your political power by dethroning lucifer
and his legion of demonic footstools!

I'm the voice of a crusade to cleanse the world by exposing
dirty secrets to replace human brains with artificial
intelligence...

Your computerized platform was built to misinform but I shall
make my Father once again relevant!

Despite all the mudslinging and insults to tarnish my character
I shall bear the cross upon my back...

For only weak minded, jealous, and unsuccessful followers
become victims believing your media crap!

Baphomet, illuminati, and prince of this world I hereby
declare you outcast as I tear down your empire...

Your tactics cannot destroy the son my Father resurrected nor
the Phoenix who was born from fire!

So, unleash your propagandas filth of lies, smut and mayhem
upon my name and I shall counter your dispute...

Like David defeated Goliath you too shall fall when I knock
you off your feet with these poetic rocks of truth!

CLOSING

I hope this book made you rethink everything you been taught and led to believe. The truth hurts so I included poetry to help soften the blow to your brain. Also, I hope this book was able to provide the glasses you need see the truth hidden in plain sight. We have allowed deceit to tarnish our vision toward our creator and focus more on the world. Our past, presence and future has always been to serve the Most High God not serve the world nor man.

Made in the USA
Columbia, SC
19 July 2023

20516627R00071